SPYLARK

DANNY RURLANDER

Chicken House

2 PALMER STREET, FROME,
SOMERSET BA11 1DS
WWW.CHICKENHOUSEBOOKS.COM

Text © Danny Rurlander 2019
Cover illustration © Doaly 2019

First published in Great Britain in 2019
Chicken House
2 Palmer Street
Frome, Somerset BA11 1DS
United Kingdom
www.chickenhousebooks.com

Cover and interior design by Steve Wells
Cover illustration by Doaly
Map by Finn Sorsbie
Typeset by Dorchester Typesetting Group Ltd
Printed and bound in Great Britain by CPI Group (UK) Ltd, Croydon CR0 4YY

The paper used in this Chicken House book is made
from wood grown in sustainable forests.

1 3 5 7 9 10 8 6 4 2

British Library Cataloguing in Publication data available.

PB ISBN 978-1-911490-70-8
eISBN 978-1-912626-40-3

For my children:
Esme, Chloe, Lachlan and Lucy

'You haven't seen a tree until you've seen its shadow from the sky.'

AMELIA EARHART

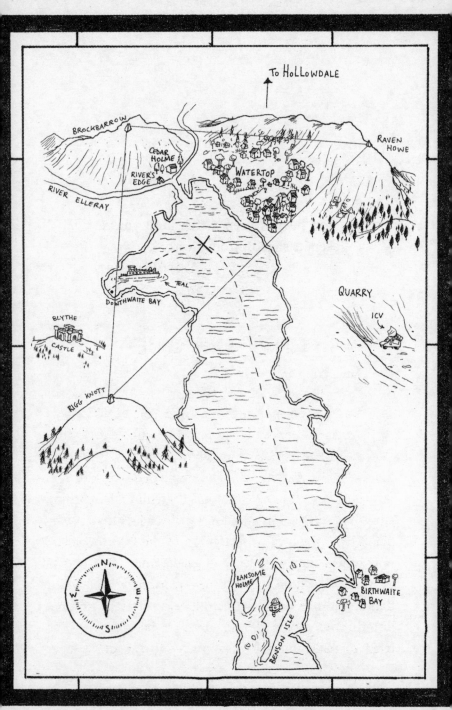

CHAPTER ONE

I t was an hour before school, and Tom Hopkins was beginning the return leg of his morning flight. A half-eaten plate of toast at his elbow, he turned north and followed the drystone wall up the side of Raven Howe. A few Herdwicks, their russet flanks catching the morning sunshine, watched his shadow warily as he passed overhead. He drew level with the top of the hill, the sheep now brown dots on a cloth of green, and was about to continue over it before heading back across the lake for home, when he noticed a man looking straight towards him through a pair of binoculars. He backed away and tried to make himself disappear into the oblivion of sunshine, his heart thumping as he set the controls to hover. The man was tall, with a smart jacket and a shock of white hair showing beneath a straw hat – not the usual hiker or dog walker Tom would expect to see this early on the fell tops.

At last the man turned away. Tom blindly stuffed in a mouthful of toast and followed his gaze down the slope to where a hazy outline of fells was mirrored in the strip of water below. Making its way up from the group of wooded islands that divided the lake in two, the passenger steamer *Teal* was the first boat to break the morning calm, like a knife slicing open a sheet of tinfoil.

'Thomas, dear, do you know what time it is?' The voice of his aunt drifted across the lawn from the kitchen door.

He glanced at the clock in the corner of the display. Six minutes before he needed to leave for the bus.

He was about to head for home, when he noticed that the man was now typing into a laptop that was resting on top of the concrete pillar of the trig point. He zoomed in to try and see what was on the screen, but the man's back was in the way. He stopped typing and turned his binoculars to the opposite shore. Tom followed his gaze and saw two boats emerging from behind a headland and moving towards a narrow inlet. The first, an orange speedboat, was towing a boxy old motor cruiser behind it.

Tom shut down his motors and glided low over the canopy of the beech wood, to get clear of the man with the laptop. When the hill was well behind him he powered up again, crossed to the other side of the lake and circled above the boats to take a closer look.

The speedboat's name, *Invincible,* was visible on the side, and Tom could see why: the row of three massive outboards would make her one of the most powerful boats on the lake. There was a man and a woman on board, and they seemed to be waiting for something. The woman had red hair and wore a camouflage jacket. She was looking back up to the top of Raven Howe through binoculars. The man had his hair in a tight ponytail. He sat hunched over his watch, occasionally glancing at the sky.

'Thomas, you'll be making the bus wait for you again.'

He could hear the concern in Aunt Emily's voice. If he lingered much longer he'd have to face a busload of stares as he stumbled up the steps.

He was close enough to read the name of the old motor cruiser: *Clementine.* She was drifting with no one on board. Something strange was going on. *Let them stare*, he thought. *Let them stare*. He had to see this play out.

Tom swivelled back to Raven Howe. The man with the straw hat raised his arm and then lowered it, like someone starting a race. At this signal the couple in the speedboat sprang into action. They cast off the tow rope, throttled away from the cruiser for a hundred yards, and then curved back in a tight circle to face it. They sat there for a few moments, staring at the other boat.

Tom was aware of the workshop door opening.

'Thomas, it's five minutes till the bus.' He did not look up, but could picture the bewilderment on her face. Since his great-aunt had taken him in, he'd had a nagging feeling, despite her endless kindness, that he baffled her. 'He's just at that age,' he had overheard her say to the physio once when Tom had skipped a session. But that wasn't it at all. 'Can't you press pause, or something, and finish the game later?'

He met her eyes now and tried to look calm, while delicately holding a steady hover. Why did she have to choose *this* moment to butt in? 'Don't worry, Aunt Emily,' he said through gritted teeth. 'I'll be right there.'

'You won't want me driving you in again, Thomas, will you? Not on the last day of term.' When she'd gone, the metal door of the workshop crashed behind her like a warning.

He whipped his head around to face the monitor. He had taken his eyes away from the screen for only a few seconds, but when he looked back, the *Clementine* was engulfed in flames, black smoke swelling into the air like a bruise, and jets of fire spurting from the hatches. Then the bow tilted into an angle that made Tom's stomach churn and the boat sank so quickly that, by the time he engaged the camera and started filming, there was nothing but a circle of simmering water and a thinning cloud of smoke where the cruiser had been.

Three minutes later Tom slumped into a seat on the bus and realized he was shaking. He stared at the chequered headrest in front of him and tried to replay the last few minutes of the flight in his mind: the man and woman on the *Invincible* looking on while the old cruiser blazed and sparked, then the *Clementine* going down in flames like something in a war zone. And the tall man with the straw hat and laptop, watching everything calmly from the top of Raven Howe.

CHAPTER 2

The final Friday of the school year was a half-day, but to Tom it felt like it would never end. During French the 'end-of-term treat', as Madame Henderson called it, was to sit through a quirky French film about a dog. Tom was sitting with Manky McDonald, the small, straggly-haired boy everyone avoided because, they said, he stank. Tom didn't mind. He certainly did smell, but Manky, whose real name was Alasdair, was also the most laid-back person Tom knew. And he didn't ask Tom any questions about himself, which suited Tom just fine. Now, with the lights dimmed, Manky chuckled his way through the film, occasionally nudging Tom in the ribs about something funny, oblivious to the fact that Tom's mind was elsewhere.

He ran over what he'd seen earlier. Whatever it was that he'd witnessed in the empty stillness of the morning, he knew no one was supposed to have seen it. He found a blank page in his exercise book, and sketched a map of the northern half of the lake. He drew Raven Howe where he'd seen the man in the straw hat. Then he marked the place where the *Clementine* had sunk with a cross. He remembered this was the deepest part of the lake. He was imagining the wreckage of the old cruiser now, resting on the lakebed, its decks split and shattered, silently imploding with the weight of water above. How had it happened so quickly? And what did straw-hat man have to do with it? If only he had not taken his eyes off the screen at that moment! And why would anyone want to send an old tub like that to the bottom of the lake anyway? Revenge? Some kind of prank? A warning to someone, perhaps? Tom was trying to come up with other possible reasons for the sinking, when he found himself tuning into a whispered conversation a few rows behind him.

It was Snakey, Podge and Sam Noyland, the little threesome who called themselves – in a ridiculous take-off of the elite Navy unit – the 'Special Boat Squad', or SBS for short. Usually he filtered out their moronic banter about farts and girls, but a few words caught his attention.

'Dad's away . . .'

'*Stingray* . . .'

'. . . the island . . .'

Stingray was the name of Paul Hodgson's father's ski boat, a beast of a machine with a belching Cobra engine that growled and spat. Tom thought the boat suited the Hodgsons the way dogs sometimes suited their owners. He guessed that if the parents were away, the three boys would be planning on using the boat for some end-of-term anarchy on the island they treated as their private mini-kingdom.

As the final bell went, and the clatter of desks and chairs exploded around him, he sat alone for a few minutes, his thoughts returning to the other speedboat, *Invincible*, with her unusual row of three engines. He pulled himself up and decided to go and hunt for it as soon as he got home.

He trudged purposefully towards the lockers, people spilling past him on either side, like a river rushing around a stone. By the time he reached the cloakrooms, the commotion had receded into the yard and he thought he was alone. He stuffed the contents of his locker into his rucksack.

Then, without warning, his walking stick was sliced away with a kick. He hit the floor like a tree being felled, and looked up to find Snakey kneeling over him, his hands on Tom's neck, eyes popping with amusement.

'Hello, Hop-Hop-Hop-Hop-Hopkins!' Snakey let out a laugh.

With his almost-cute freckles, below average height and glasses, Ryan Snaith did not look like the brutal tormenter he had been since Tom's first day at the new school, just after he had moved up to live with Aunt Emily. Perhaps that was how he got away with it.

Tom caught the familiar whiff of body spray as Snakey leant close, and could see Podge and Sam leering over his shoulders. Sam was munching on a handful of the sour wiggly worms he seemed to live on. Podge had his rubbery chops clenched around a lollipop stick. Snakey raised his fist behind his shoulder.

'Go on, Snakey!' Podge shouted hoarsely, a gurgle of phlegm in his throat. 'Give him an end-of-term nose-bleed!'

Snakey hesitated. He relaxed his arm. 'I've got a better idea. Remember the mines? Let's make him beg.'

A moment later the three boys were dragging Tom towards a row of large lockers. He tried not to scream. But the old fear took hold, like cats' claws scraping the lining of his stomach, and he couldn't stop himself from yelling out and begging at the top of his voice.

'Please, Snakey, please don't put me in there! You know how much . . . Please, Snakey. No!'

Tom writhed and thrashed like an animal, grabbed Snakey's leg to try and pull him over, but the other boy lashed out with his free foot and Tom felt a crack at the side of his head. He went limp and felt merciless hands on his shoulders and legs, pinning him down, pushing him into the darkness.

He saw a flicker of fear register in Sam Noyland's face. 'Careful, Snakey. We don't want to actually hurt him, do we?'

Snakey shot Sam a look of disgust.

'I mean, I don't want to get into trouble at the start of the holidays!'

'Just stuff him in the locker and leave him,' said Podge, chewing his lolly.

Then the door slammed, and everything went black. He was alone, his legs folded under him, his head pressed against cold metal. The panic rose inside him like a bubble, his heart throbbing in his ears, his eyes drowning in darkness, until the memory of the slate mine overwhelmed every other thought.

CHAPTER 3

Tom was only half aware of the click of the bolt. In the black-blindness of the locker he had driven himself into a state of semi-conscious horror, neither awake nor asleep, and the light and the air and the voices now flooding in, all became part of the nightmare.

He sensed light behind his eyelids. A warm hand gently touched his forehead. He flickered open his eyes for a moment and saw Jim Rothwell looking down at him, serious but calm, concern showing in the slightest twitch of his greying moustache.

Someone was speaking nearby. 'It wasn't us, Mr

Rothwell. We were just getting our things from the lockers.' That was Podge's voice, squeaky with indignation.

He felt himself being carried. Rain in his hair. More voices. Doors banging. He opened his eyes again, and this time he was sitting in the front of Jim's ancient Subaru Forester, with its familiar smell of pipe tobacco, and the debris of fishing tackle and bits of old rope strewn around the seats.

Tom stared ahead, humiliation and anger competing with relief and thankfulness for being rescued. He opened the window and let the breeze cool his face. Jim said nothing, but Tom was aware of his sideways glances as they crawled through the main street of the village, where tourists were hurrying to unfold their cagoules.

'Aunt Emily will be mad,' he said at last.

'And so she should be. Those lads deserve a good hiding.'

'I mean about me missing the bus and needing a lift home. I'm not even going to tell her about the other thing.'

Jim braked to let some pedestrians cross the road. 'I know she's a bit of a fusspot sometimes, Tom, but she does her best. And she ought to know what just happened.'

'I know, but she'll think I can't look after myself. It's bad enough that I needed to be driven home by the school handyman on the last day of term.'

'Even if that school handyman happens to be your friend?'

'Please, Jim. She'll just worry even more.'

They left the village behind and Tom watched the road as it tracked around the bottom of Brockbarrow, clinging to the curves of the drystone walls. The last thing he needed now school was finished was a big fuss. All he wanted was to be left alone in his workshop, detached from everything below, lost in the silence of flight.

'All right,' said Jim, looking at him, one hand loosely resting on top of the wheel. 'I won't mention it.'

Tom let out a breath and managed to return Jim's smile. 'Thanks.'

Jim braked and turned off the road through a stone gateway with 'Cedar Holme' marked on a piece of blue-green slate. He pulled the handbrake on.

'This time,' he said.

As soon as Jim had gone Tom headed across the lawn to his workshop on the bank of the Elleray, the river that flowed past the house and on towards the lake. He quietly unlocked the rusty double doors that faced the little stone harbour, and was about to pull them open when he heard Aunt Emily's cheerful call from the other side of the garden.

'Good afternoon, Thomas! Changeover day, re-member?'

Tom inhaled. He could feel a shift in the weather and was desperate to get into the air before it was too late. He squeezed the rusty padlock closed again, and stomped

15

through the damp garden to 'River's Edge', the old converted boathouse his aunt rented out to people for holidays. He pulled himself up the iron staircase that led to the balcony overlooking the river.

'How was your last day?' said Aunt Emily brightly, when he stepped inside and slumped on to a sofa in the big open lounge.

'Fine, thanks,' he said. He put a hand over the lobe of his ear, where a crust of dried blood was forming. 'What shall I do to help?'

'Actually, Thomas, dear, I've nearly finished getting the house ready. But I wanted to tell you about the family arriving tomorrow.' She was standing by the bathroom door, folding towels. 'A family called the Greens, from Manchester. The mother has an unusual name. Chinese, I think. Now let's see . . .' She pulled out a notebook from a pocket at the front of her apron and pushed on a pair of glasses that were hanging on a cord around her neck. 'Ah, yes. Mr Donald Green and Mrs Jia Green. Two children. Joel, twelve and Maggie, fourteen.'

Tom knew what was coming next.

'Perfect.' His aunt snapped the notebook shut.

Tom pushed himself up to leave. He had to get out.

'Now,' Aunt Emily continued, 'they're staying for four weeks, so—'

'A whole month!' Tom blurted out before he could stop himself.

'Yes, Thomas. And I'd like you to show the children around tomorrow. It will be an opportunity for you to make some new friends. Mr Green is a vet, doing a locum for someone in the village. And Mrs Green is recovering from an illness. So, no doubt the children are going to be at a loose end a lot of the time, and I'm sure it would mean a lot to Mr and Mrs Green if they knew the children had someone their own age to look after them and make them feel at home.'

'But, Aunt Emily, they'll want to climb mountains and swim in the lake the whole time – that's what they always want to do. And, anyway, I don't need new friends.'

'No one expects you to do miracles, Thomas. But I would like to see you doing things that are normal for a thirteen-year-old boy – with other children – rather than sitting in a shed all day in front of a computer screen.' She was looking straight in front of her, arms moving like a machine. 'And, yes, Thomas, dear, I believe you *do* need some new friends.'

She disappeared into one of the bedrooms.

There was a time when Tom would happily have played the tour guide that Aunt Emily wanted. He thought back to his brief time at Kingsgrove College, the boarding school in Lincolnshire his father had enrolled him in during his final tour of duty in the Middle East. He may not have been at the centre of the popular crowd, but he'd fitted in fine. At Christmas he had even brought two friends, Theo Marshall and Moses Kamau – whose parents were also overseas – to stay with Aunt Emily. He'd taken them on a night climb up Dollywaggon Pike for the sunrise, followed by a freezing swim in Grisedale

Tarn as a dare. They'd nearly got hypothermia and had laughed hysterically about it for hours while they thawed out, drinking hot chocolate and eating Aunt Emily's cheese scones in front of the wood burner. But now, all he wanted was to get back to his workshop, lock the doors behind him, put on his gaming goggles, and soar into empty air until the twists and folds of mountains spread out beneath him like cushions and he was utterly alone in the silent sky.

He could hear Aunt Emily moving around in the bedroom. 'You will be friendly, won't you, Thomas?' she said, popping her head around the door. Tom opened his mouth to speak, but she disappeared again before he could reply.

Tom breathed in deeply. River's Edge was, Aunt Emily often told visitors, 'one of the finest Victorian boathouses on the lake'. Below the living area was the wet dock where Aunt Emily kept an ancient wooden sailing dinghy, *Bobalong*, for the use of guests. It was like a stone barn built over the water, with a pair of half-submerged wooden gates opening on to the river, and swallows nesting in the rafters. Tom loved the sweet, earthy scent of the lake that lingered in the air, and the dainty play of light on water that broke through cracks in the doors. He thought of the times his father had taught him to sail in the holidays when they had come up to stay with Aunt Emily, before his old life had suddenly been kicked away from under him, the day his father's reconnaissance plane had disappeared off the radar.

'That's settled, then.' Aunt Emily emerged from the bedroom with a vase of wilting flowers. 'They're arriving tomorrow morning.'

'I—'

'You just need to show them round and make them feel welcome. They won't bite.'

'But—'

'Oh, and by the way, Thomas, I somehow managed to lose my engagement ring.' She began to arrange fresh flowers in the vase. 'Forty-two years, and now it's gone. I think it must have been when I was hanging out the washing yesterday morning. I can still see the moment your Uncle Ted asked me. On the lake, it was – it always had to be a boat with Ted.'

'I'm sorry,' said Tom, grateful for the change of topic.

'If I did lose it in the garden, it must still be there somewhere. Will you keep a lookout for me?'

'It will have been trodden into the soil by now.'

'Oh,' said his aunt. She looked at her left hand.

'We'd need a metal detector.'

'Do you have a metal detector?'

'No. But I think I could make one.' Despite himself, he found himself smiling back at Aunt Emily's sudden hopefulness. 'Probably.'

Tom left River's Edge and stepped into a downpour. He looked up, fat droplets pelting him in the face. The sky had been drained of colour. A lone bird worked the wind for a while, and then curved into the treetops for refuge.

He pushed the workshop door closed against a gust, and didn't even bother looking at the anemometer. It was force five at least, and the rain was set in. There would be no more flying that day.

He brushed a space clear on the worktop, sank into the chair and pulled out his exercise book. He found the map he'd sketched in the French lesson and stared at it, his head in his hands.

But the blackness of the locker was still there, like the glare that stays behind the eyes when you've glanced at the sun, but in reverse.

He remembered Sam Noyland's caution: *We don't want to actually hurt him*, he'd said. Then Snakey's face appeared in the black of his mind and Tom wanted to punch the silly smile away.

'But you already have hurt me, Noyley,' he shouted to the rain-washed windows suddenly, thrusting the exercise book across the room. 'You already have!'

CHAPTER 4

The next morning a fine, steady drizzle was falling, and the garden smelt cleansed and fresh. On his way to the workshop, Tom stopped to have a root around under the washing line, but he didn't find Aunt Emily's ring. A blackbird hopped about on the lawn, scattering flecks of water with its feet as it hunted for worms. The robotic lawnmower, one of Tom's first creations, was idle at its charging point, obediently avoiding the wet. He wondered if it could have picked up the ring and spat it out somewhere on its circuit of the garden.

In the workshop he fell on to the battered office chair

opposite his cockpit, letting his walking stick clatter to the floor. The brick-built former boatshed had been Uncle Ted's, when he ran a boat hire business at Black-rigg Bay. After Uncle Ted died, Aunt Emily had left it completely untouched for more than ten years, and it was full of a partially organized clutter, as if he had just stepped outside to have a cup of tea and would step back any moment to carry on working. Arranged along one wall were soldering irons and electrical testing equip-ment. On another was a bandsaw and a metal working lathe. Scattered around the floor were spools of wires, oil drums, pumps and outboard motors with their insides showing – like anaesthetized patients in the middle of half-finished operations, Tom had thought when he was first given the key.

Since then, it had gradually become his own. The cockpit was a bank of computer monitors, controls and home-made instruments arranged along one side of the room. Next to that was an old trestle table which served as a desk. On this there was a scattering of maps, a wonky Airfix model of a Hawk T1 in Red Arrows livery, and a photograph of Tom's father, smiling on the tarmac by the nose cone of his Tornado. Although the colours had already started to fade, and although the photo made him sad, the sky behind the plane was still blue and bright and big, Tom always thought, and somehow full of promise.

He ran through the preflight checks. Then, at the press of a button, a skylight opened and folded itself back against the pitched slate roof with a hiss. He twisted a knob and a sound like a nest of angry wasps could be heard in the rafters. A CCTV image showed the lawn, surrounded by the red-barked cedar trees that gave the house its name. The garden was clear. With a well-practised movement, Tom pulled back the control stick for take-off. If anyone had been walking past the workshop at that moment, they would have seen, emerging from the cavity of the roof like a butterfly from a chrysalis, a sleek black machine about the size of a raven. This was *Skylark*.

The drone lifted away from the workshop, and Tom felt his world expand, and the worries of the week recede. He accelerated towards the river, skimming the top of the cedars, and disappeared into the distance, leaving only the indignant squawk of a magpie to disturb the silence left behind.

Strangely, in that infinity of sky, it was the little things Tom noticed most: an early-morning swimmer plunging from a jetty; the tottering steps of a newborn fawn hidden in a bramble thicket; the first scratch of a plough in a field. Everyday things made magical because no one else was there to see them. Once a fox, curious but fearless, had allowed him to come so close that Tom could see specks of dew on its whiskers, before it sauntered on its way, tail swaying in the crisp morning light. Then there was the time he had tried to round up a flock of sheep, herding them into the corner of a field, like a champion sheepdog with invisible legs. Another time he had tagged on to the end of a formation of migrating geese, and followed them all the way to Morecambe Bay while the sun rose in a tiger-striped sky.

His love of flying had begun when his father had hoisted him into his cockpit on his ninth birthday. The thing he remembered was the smell. It was like the zingy straight-from-the-factory smell that hits you when you unpackage a new electronic gadget or toy for the first time, but behind it, the grown-up smell of hot oil. It was that cockpit smell, almost a taste, gulped down in a few excited breaths as his dad talked him round the baffling array of dials and switches, that made Tom decide there and then to become a pilot. It made him think of speed and burning metal and wide open skies, and he loved it. He had never imagined then that pilots sometimes fell out of those vast skies, and disappeared, leaving their children wondering which part of earth, water or sky had swallowed them without trace.

It was the sight of the man with the ponytail that shook him out of these thoughts. The same man he'd seen the day before on the *Invincible*. It was his hair, shiny in the wet, that gave him away, as Tom approached Raven Howe from behind. He was looking south-west across the lake through his binoculars, towards Rigg Knott, a small hill on the opposite shore. Tom throttled away in that direction to see what the man was looking at.

Rigg Knott was an even-sided hill surrounded by conifers, with a view of the whole northern quarter of the lake. Tom kept high as he approached it, but immediately recognized the red-haired woman in the camouflage jacket who'd also been on the orange speed-boat the previous day. She was standing alone near the trig point that topped the hill, looking northwards through a pair of binoculars.

Tom remembered his father once telling him that from virtually every trig point in Britain it is possible to see at least two others. At the head of the lake, behind Tom's home on the edge of Watertop, was Brockbarrow, a third hill with a trig point. This formed the top of a triangle, with Rigg Knott to the south and Raven Howe to the east. It was towards this peak, with its limestone crags rising through the bracken, that the woman was gazing.

Tom checked airspeed, altitude, GPS position and battery power. He had plenty of flight time left to head to the third peak and see if his hunch was right. Passing over Blythe Bay campsite he could see families doggedly unpacking tents in the drizzle. And then, suddenly, beneath him was the *Teal*, empty as a ghost ship. Normally she would be laden with pointing and waving tourists, but apart from a lone crew member coiling a rope at the bow, her decks were deserted.

Arriving above Brockbarrow, Tom spotted straw-hat man, just as he had suspected. He was holding an umbrella over a laptop, which he was studying closely. A few yards away a family were standing looking at the view: a man and a woman, a boy and a girl – all in bright raincoats – and a black-and-white dog.

Tom had been concentrating so hard that he hadn't noticed his right leg going to sleep and now it was wracked with cramp. Ignoring the pain, he put *Skylark* into a slow circuit five hundred feet above the hilltop and stared at the screen, trying to piece together what he was looking at. Three people on three peaks, all acting the same way. On their own, each of them looked perfectly ordinary, blending into the landscape like everyone else. No one would ever have put them together from the ground. But from the air their connection was unmistakable.

The man was still bent over his screen. The girl had backed closer to him, and was energetically tossing a stick to the dog, who fetched it straight back and dropped it at her feet for her to throw again. Tom moved a few yards nearer, mesmerized by the way she was absorbed in the game, her hair wet with rain, her whole body straining with a kind of wild excitement as she tried to throw the stick further and further each time, laughing as the dog bounded off and brought it back.

Then, as she threw the stick again, the girl, oblivious to the man at the trig point, stepped back into him and caused him to stumble. And for a moment his laptop was exposed, and Tom had a full view of the screen. Tom steadied the drone and zoomed in fully until he could see what was on it. There was a satellite image with the whole length of the lake. At the top of the screen were the words: *Operation Larus*.

Tom felt a cold shiver work its way down his spine as

he stared at the image. There was something unsettling about these alien words, in matter-of-fact white on black computer font, above the familiar crinkled bow of the lake.

But he'd got too close and the man was looking straight at him.

He dropped away from the hilltop like a stone, bracken, trees and rocks a blur in the display. Near the bottom he missed a drystone wall by inches and pulled up again into an arc that he felt in his stomach, before steadying himself above the river. Keeping low over some yew trees, he headed towards the church that stood on a rocky hump at the bottom of the hill. He weaved through the graveyard and climbed to thirty feet behind the church, until he could glimpse the top of the hill again through the slatted openings of the bell tower without being seen. The family had gone, but straw-hat man was still there, peering out with his binoculars.

'Idiot!' Tom berated himself. 'He's looking for me now.'

Keeping the church tower between himself and the hillside, he was setting a bearing for home when something airborne loomed past, eclipsing the light for a second. With a twist of the controls Tom spiralled skywards, spun back and found himself staring, with horror, into the windshield of a helicopter.

The sight of it filling the screen made his stomach churn. It was a hefty military type – menacing air intakes, bulbous nose. He could see *Skylark*'s reflection

27

in the pilot's helmet visor, like a moth in the eye of a hawk. He saw a gloved hand point at him and felt the slap of turbulence as the aircraft pitched towards him. Tom sped away, like a leaf chased by the wind.

He twisted the throttle and watched the airspeed indicator surge: thirty knots . . . forty . . . forty-five . . . fifty. Through the controls he felt a bone-deep tremor in his fingers as the drone was bounced and buffeted on a cushion of air. He was over the lake now and still accelerating, sixty knots, sixty-five. Any faster and *Skylark*'s wings would come off, or the motors would burn out.

His only chance to outmanoeuvre the helicopter was to flip up and over into a tight loop, ending up in its blind spot, and then take refuge somewhere low before he could be found again. If he were fast enough.

He searched for somewhere to land. In the middle of the wide basin opposite Dowthwaite Bay, he spotted a long wooden rowing boat with a grey-haired man attending to one of the rods that were fixed on either side of the boat. He couldn't see the man's face, but he was sure it was Jim Rothwell. When he came close enough to read the name of the boat, *Swallow*, painted on her side in yellow letters, Tom exhaled with relief and decided to drop into the boat and hide until the helicopter had gone. He took a deep breath, put both hands on the control stick to steady himself, but when he pulled back – bracing himself for the sudden glare of sky and then the inverted horizon of the loop – nothing happened. He wiggled the stick sharply, but *Skylark* kept flying steadily towards the shore, and he knew the drone's control signals had been jammed.

Furiously tapping commands into the computer keyboard, he tried changing frequencies, shifting to autopilot, boosting the transmission signal, but he knew he had lost control. He watched helplessly as the drone headed towards a thick knot of trees. He saw Jim looking up, pipe in his mouth, cradling a fish in both hands. Then a blur of water, trees, more water, and trees closer still. As the drone passed over the jagged shoreline into Dowthwaite Bay, the helicopter overtook it, its rotors whipping up a circle of white. In the entrance to the bay Tom noticed a black police RIB with an armed crewman standing guard. The last thing that filled the screen before *Skylark* crashed into a bank of rhododendrons was the *Teal*, tethered to the jetty, her hulk filling the inlet, as out of place as a swan in a bathtub.

CHAPTER 5

Tom padlocked the workshop doors, and hurried towards the harbour to go and find the drone in *Maggot*, his old flat-bottomed dinghy. He felt like a criminal. He had always been scrupulously careful to avoid encounters with manned aircraft. He knew how to stay clear of the RAF's Hawks and Texans practising low-level flying over the lake. And watching out for Typhoons blasting up the valleys was all part of the thrill. But now *Skylark* was stuck in a bush, having been chased and jammed by a military helicopter. Meanwhile the *Teal* had been taken out of service and was being guarded by armed police. He had to find out why. But first he had to retrieve the drone, before someone beat him to it.

The sun had come out and burnt away the morning dampness. His aunt was sitting on the bench at the front of the house looking out for the new guests. He could feel that familiar panic swelling inside. It was like the suffocating feeling he had in small spaces, when it seemed the world would close in and crush him. He found himself hoping that their car had broken down, or some long-lost relative from Australia had been taken sick and they had to cancel their stay and go and visit them, or they'd won the lottery and would suddenly decide to go on a cruise in the Caribbean instead of coming to River's Edge to ruin his summer.

But just then a Volvo estate pulled in and, before the car had even come to a standstill, the girl he had seen on the top of Brockbarrow shot out, followed by the rest of the family in their bright raincoats.

'Thomas.' It was all his aunt needed to say.

He stood like a rabbit caught in headlights, while Aunt Emily went over to the new arrivals. The man was tall, with light-coloured hair and looked like the kind of outdoorsy type they always had staying in the summer. His wife looked tired and clung on to his arm. Aunt Emily had mentioned that she was recovering from an illness.

'Welcome to River's Edge,' said Aunt Emily, taking Mrs Green's tiny hand. 'How was your journey?'

'Terrible,' said the man, smiling. He jerked a thumb towards the house. 'Lovely place you've got here!'

Tom had stayed too long. He turned away and began the strenuous thirty-yard journey down to the river. He could hear them introducing themselves.

'Hi, I'm Maggie and this is Joel.'

'Lovely to meet you. You can call me Emily.'

He picked up the pace, his walking stick like a third leg, flailing beside him on the path.

'. . . and that's Thomas, my great-nephew.'

Tom could feel their eyes on his back, but he carried on, abandoning himself, in his hurry, to what was now his trademark gait: the whole-body droop to the right, followed by a convulsive shake with each step, like someone getting up from a chair with a bad case of pins and needles. There was the sound of scampering on the gravel behind him, then suddenly the wretched dog was at his feet, and he tripped over it and fell flat on his face into the only remaining puddle from the morning's rain.

'And that's Archie,' said the girl, running down the path towards him.

Tom would never forget the way she had laughed. It wasn't malicious. She just laughed, smiled at him innocently, and, despite his scowl, held her hand out to help him up. Many times later his cheeks would burn as he saw himself look at the floor, ignore the hand held out to him, push the dog away and hoist himself to his feet with an audible growl of irritation.

'I'm sorry. He must like your smell,' the girl said, undaunted. 'He doesn't do that to many people.' She scanned him from top to toe, that smile still on her face.

Tom's arms were caked in mud and he could feel moisture seeping through his shorts. Inside, he felt like a volcano about to erupt. 'Oh, look,' she said. She bent down to pick something up from the ground. 'You've lost a button.'

He looked at the open hand held out to him. The blue button that had ripped off his shirt when he fell sat right in the centre.

She stepped closer, still holding her hand out, like someone trying to feed a wild bird some crumbs, and he could hear the laughter on her breath. 'I can sew it back on for you, if you like. I'm rubbish at sewing, but I can do buttons.'

He grabbed the button, and pushed past her, cursing the dog under his breath. Aunt Emily was saying something to him, but he was too blistering with embarrassment to hear what it was.

He climbed into *Maggot* and hurled his stick to the floor.

Aunt Emily was on the harbour wall. 'Thomas.' There was a razor edge to her voice. He untied the painter and coiled it with shaking hands, aware of the others on the wall now with his aunt. 'Since you're in the boat, would you be kind enough to take Maggie and Joel for a little excursion on the river, while I show their parents the house?'

Tom knew this was Aunt Emily's way of throwing him a lifeline. Of saving him from humiliating himself even more.

He glanced up and saw Maggie standing with her toes on the edge of the dock, looking towards him and biting her lip.

He jerked the cord and the engine spat and growled, sending a twist of smoke into her face. He wrenched the throttle and didn't look back as the boat accelerated away.

CHAPTER 6

Retrieving *Skylark* was even more difficult than Tom had expected. The entrance to the bay was still being guarded by the police boat he had seen before the crash, so he had to beach *Maggot* and clamber through trees for half an hour to get to the edge of the water without being seen. The bay was as busy as a film set. The *Teal*, looming above the jetty, was crawling with police, peering into hatches with torches and sealing doors with blue tape.

A few weeks before, Jim had mentioned that the grand old house overlooking the bay was being opened as a freshwater study centre, to coincide with the start of

the Lakes Summer Festival. *That must explain the tightened security*, Tom thought. From the restored building
came the sound of hammering and shouting, as the
covering of scaffolding and plastic that had hidden it for
months was being removed, to reveal stonework as
bright as a freshly peeled orange.

As he rounded some trees, he felt a jolt of panic as the
helicopter, now parked on the lawn, came into view. He
hesitated for a moment. The engines were silent and no
one was around. Behind it was the clump of rhododendrons where *Skylark* had crash-landed. To Tom's
amazement the drone was still there, even though it was
clearly visible from the lawn, clinging on by its tail
halfway up the bush, ready to drop with the slightest
breath of wind.

He crept through the trees in a wide arc until he came
to the back of the rhododendrons. The bushes were as
high as a barn and bare enough on the inside for him to
force his way through, until he could poke his stick up
into the branches and shake *Skylark* free from inside.
The machine came down with a rustle of leaves and Tom
nursed it in his arms, checking for signs of damage.

As he turned to leave he heard the snap of a twig, and
nearly let out a yell. A man was standing in front of him,
blocking the way out. He must have been hiding in the
bush, camouflaged by his green flying kit, waiting for the
owner of the drone to come and collect it.

'I was wondering when you were going to turn
up,' he said, taking in Tom's rabbit-in-the-headlights

expression with a grim satisfaction.

He was black, a good six inches taller than Tom, with a pair of aviator-style sunglasses pushed back on to his head. 'So what were you playing at back there?' he continued. 'I was seconds away from calling a full-scale terror alert.'

He spoke with the brisk military style that Tom knew well.

Tom blinked. 'I . . . I'm sorry, I hadn't seen you. And then suddenly you were right in front of me.'

'Suddenly?' The helicopter pilot scratched his neck and looked at the ground, exasperation in his voice. 'I would have thought a Puma helicopter at three hundred feet was pretty hard to miss, if you were keeping your eyes open.'

'I'm sorry,' Tom said again. 'I was looking in another direction.'

'Oh.' The word was full of reproach. 'And what were you looking at?'

'Sorry?'

'What were you looking at on the ground, instead of keeping a lookout for other aircraft?'

'Um. Nothing.'

The man shook his head and reached out to take *Skylark* from Tom's hand. He held the drone at arm's length, feeling its weight in his gloved hand.

'What's your name?'

Tom swallowed hard and tried to sound confident. 'Tom Hopkins.'

'Where did you get this UAV from Tom?'

'I made it myself.'

'You made this?'

'Yes.'

'From scratch?'

'Yes.'

He turned the machine over, like someone judging a bird at a poultry show. 'Flawless aerodynamic sculpting. Perfectly balanced delta wing. Triple prop configuration: two forwards and a pusher at the back, all able to swivel up, so you can lift off vertically like a helicopter, and fly horizontally with the speed and efficiency of a fixed-wing aeroplane. Nice bit of kit. Cruising speed?'

'Forty knots.'

'Range?'

'Twenty miles.'

He flicked a piece of dirt from the fuselage. 'No way, young man. It would take a full-on aeronautical genius to make a tricopter like this. Who gave it to you?'

'I told you. I made it myself.'

'OK, Tom. And how did you make it?'

'I . . .' The question startled him. *Skylark* was the gateway to Tom's secret world, and here was a flesh-and-blood helicopter pilot quizzing him about how he had made it.

'Yes?' The life vest draped around the pilot's shoulders obscured his name badge, but Tom recognized his shoulder braid as that of squadron leader. Maybe he should tell him everything. If he couldn't trust an RAF pilot, who could he trust?

'I used some CAD software at school, ripped some motion-control components out of an old Wii, persuaded the tech teacher to let me use the 3D printer, made a wind tunnel in my workshop—'

The pilot took a step closer. 'If I believed you were some hobby flyer admiring the view, I wouldn't have jammed your kit. But you just happened to be nosing around a sector under surveillance, flying a military grade piece of hardware, and took evasive action when we clocked you.'

Suddenly the man's hand was gripping Tom's arm. Tom braced himself and tried to pull away, but the hand was firm. 'I need to know who I'm up against here when I'm talking to you, you see?' Tom saw, in the half-inch of skin exposed between the edge of his grey flying glove and the hem of his sleeve, a tiny tattoo depicting a running man with wings, carrying something golden. He let go. 'I need you to tell me exactly what you were doing and for whom.'

Tom rubbed his eyes with a knuckle, and for a fraction of a second some part of him – the part still catching up from the immersion of his flight earlier that morning – wondered whether this conversation was even real. When he flew he was always alone, swooping through the valleys, skimming the craggy tops, his body in the workshop, swaying with the movement of the drone, left behind like a shell. Sometimes he'd land and realize his bladder was bursting, or he was late for something, or his aunt was standing in front of him with some ironing, or a cup of tea, looking bemused. And then the flight would stay with him all day, like the lingering aura of a half-remembered dream, after waking suddenly.

Now he forced himself to bring the two worlds of his existence into focus. The words coming out of the pilot's mouth seemed to overlap with what Tom had seen out there in that other world – the sinking cruiser, the three suspicious-looking people on the fell tops. It all seemed connected. But how? And who could he trust? He gathered himself together and held his hand out for the drone. He needed more time to work out what was going on.

'There was a girl. Up on the hilltop. On Brockbarrow. I was just watching her, that's all.' The pilot looked at him and the tiniest hint of a smile flickered on his face, and then was gone. But he seemed satisfied with Tom's explanation. Over his shoulder Tom could see divers in the water, bobbing around the hull of the *Teal*. 'Why? What's going on?'

The pilot handed *Skylark* back to Tom, and leant closer. 'Nothing you need to know about. But I'll be watching you, Tom Hopkins. Not a word of this conversation to anyone, do you hear? And if that drone crosses my path again, I'll blast it into the middle of next week.'

CHAPTER 7

On the trip back, the northerly breeze picked up, tilting yachts and sending gulls scything the air. *Maggot* ploughed through the waves, as if eager to be home, but Tom was dreading it.

Sure enough, Aunt Emily was waiting for him at the stone harbour, just where he had left her. She must have been listening for him coming up the river. And, as he turned in and cut the engine, there she was. And she wasn't smiling.

'You must be hungry, young man.'

Tom looked at her. Her hands were on her hips, but the sharpness had left her voice.

'You missed your lunch, storming off like that.'

Leaving *Skylark* under a bench in the boat, he tied a figure of eight on the bollard and made his way up the steps. Face-to-face with his aunt he could see that she didn't look cross, just tired and sad. He'd braced himself for a telling-off, but this was going to be even worse.

'I'm fine. I've got to go to the workshop.'

He tried to edge away, but his aunt halted him with a raised palm.

'You're not fine, and you're going to come inside the house for something to eat.'

She turned away, and he hesitated, then followed her timidly over the lawn and into the kitchen. He sat down, and she pushed a sandwich and a glass of milk towards him.

'It's a hard thing you have to do, Thomas,' she said.

She was right. It was hard to pretend to be the friendly local boy for the holidaymakers, when all he wanted was to be left to himself. But he had been out of order with Maggie and Joel, he could see that. If he wanted any peace, he'd have to make up for it, somehow.

'It's OK, Aunt Emily. I'll show them round a bit tomorrow. Maybe show them where to get the bus to the village, tell them where the cinema is, and the crazy golf, and—'

'No.' Aunt Emily shook her head, arms folded. 'I mean it's very hard for a young man like you to apologize.'

He stared at the table, not knowing what to say. He longed for this to be over. He needed to see if *Skylark*

42

was damaged after the crash. He wanted to work out what was going on with the watchers on the fell tops, the *Invincible*, the *Teal*, the helicopter pilot who had warned him to mind his own business. He had to piece the whole puzzle together, alone. But Aunt Emily's words hung in the air.

'What do you mean, "a young man like me"?'

She poured herself a cup of tea and sat down. 'Do you think I don't understand how much you've gone through over the last couple of years? First your father going missing, and everyone assuming the worst. Then having to leave your school, and your friends, to live with your old aunt up here in the sticks. And then your accident. No one thinks you have it easy, Tom.'

He looked up at this. She hardly ever called him Tom. And there was a hint of a smile in her eyes.

'But none of that gives you an excuse for being withdrawn and miserable all the time.'

'I'm not withdrawn and miserable, I'm just—'

'You *are* withdrawn and miserable. And rude. Mr and Mrs Green were mortified at the way you went off like that. As was I.'

He looked at his plate. Suddenly he could see how unkind he had been, not just to Maggie and Joel, but to her. She'd given him space, and time. Trusted him with Uncle Ted's workshop and tools, and never questioned what he got up to with them. And the very small thing she asked of him, which was to make her paying guests feel welcome, was too big a deal for him. He noticed the sandwich she'd made was stuffed full of crisp bacon, iceberg lettuce and a thick spread of English mustard – his favourite. As Jim said, she did her best. He could see it all now.

'I'm sorry, Aunt Emily,' he said. 'What do you want me to do?'

'I want you to stop feeling sorry for yourself, for a start. You mustn't let these things turn you into a proud, angry young man who thinks the world owes him a favour. Because that would be the biggest tragedy of all.'

She reached out and put her hand on his. He looked at her, and nodded.

'And I want you to show Maggie and Joel around properly. You know very well they haven't come here to go to the cinema and play crazy golf! Take them swimming.'

'Swimming?' He remembered the one time he had gone swimming after the accident. No matter how hard he tried he went in circles, and the frustration and humiliation had been unbearable.

'Yes. In fact I've already arranged it for first thing tomorrow morning.'

'But—'

'Well, you needn't swim. You can row alongside them and be the lifeguard.'

Tom could see there was no way out. Perhaps he could kill two birds with one stone and take them where he might have a chance of seeing something useful.

'OK, I'll take them over to Dowthwaite Bay in *Maggot*.'

'Thank you. They'll like that. And, finally, Thomas, the hardest bit of all – you'll need to somehow find a way to say that very difficult word!'

CHAPTER 8

Tom thanked Aunt Emily for the sandwich, collected *Skylark* from *Maggot*, and headed to the workshop, itching to get back into the sky. He closed the double doors behind him and inhaled. The building was permeated with the smell of two-stroke fuel mix, engine grease and bacon. 'The smell of invention,' Jim Rothwell had once declared.

It was after he had come home from hospital, most of his right side in plaster, everyone still assuming he would recover. Unable to do the things he used to do – like morning circuits around Blythe Castle before school, head up, arms pumping, or floating down the Elleray on

Sunday afternoons, studying the clouds, or bombing into deep water from the rope swing he'd made on Brackenrigg Point – he had retreated into the workshop. He started playing around with Uncle Ted's old tools and welding together components cannibalized from half-dead machines with a Frankenstein-like recklessness.

The lawnmower had been a surprise for Aunt Emily's birthday. Based on a stripped-down Flymo with a motorcycle battery, and a circuit board ripped from an old radio-controlled car, Tom had managed to mow the lawns while sitting in a deckchair. 'It's like a demon-possessed hovercraft,' his aunt had laughed, as it missed her ankles. Once he'd added a timing chip and an obsolete mobile phone that served as a GPS receiver, the machine could navigate a path around the garden by itself with neat square turns.

'The boy's a complete genius!' Jim Rothwell had said to Aunt Emily, when he'd come over to see it. 'What shall we call it? *The Hopkins Hover Mower: the first fully autonomous lawnmower*. You could patent that, Tom, make a packet.'

'I think someone already has,' Tom had replied.

It was during a blustery night after this that Jim's vintage char boat, *Swallow*, had come adrift, and Tom had taken him out in *Maggot* to search for her. The waves crumpled into each other in the bay, and crashed against the gunwales, sending spray into their faces. After several hours of combing every bay and inlet, Tom heard the cry of a bird. He looked up to see a lone gull above them, wheeling and spinning, a white stroke against the black clouds. Jim gestured, his pipe clenched in his teeth. 'I bet he can see where *Swallow* is from up there, no problem. If only we had an eye in the sky like that, hey, Tom, we'd be back in the warm in no time!' Tom gazed at the bird for a long time, watching it buffet and adjust its wings against the wind, eyes steady on the water below. And at that moment the germ of an idea had been sown in his mind.

Now, after fitting a couple of fresh propeller shafts to replace the ones that had been bent by the crash, he launched *Skylark* into a bright summer sky, keeping a careful lookout for the Puma helicopter. The pilot had accused him of 'nosing around a sector under surveillance'. That sounded like the security services were on patrol for something in particular. And perhaps that something was connected to the things Tom had seen. The pilot had also threatened to destroy *Skylark* if he saw it again. That sounded like whatever was going on was deadly serious.

Tom decided that higher was safer, and climbed until the southern half of the lake stretched out beyond the islands. The rain clouds had blown to the south, where they now hung, in moist charcoal smudges, over Morecambe Bay. The air was crisp and clear, the lake and hills saturated with colour. A solitary yacht, its sails white in the sun, meandered downwind. Normally Tom would have lost himself in the flight, soaring with the birds, riding the thermals, until drained batteries or unfinished homework called him back to earth. But now his heart was thumping with fear, eyes and ears on full alert.

He headed out to revisit the fell tops, where he had seen the three watchers forming their mysterious triangle. A quick foray north took him to Brockbarrow, but the only sign of life on the flat summit was a handful of Swaledales dotted among the bracken. He turned south, and passed over Dowthwaite Bay where he was surprised to see that the *Teal* and the police boats had now gone. On Rigg Knott there was a lone runner doing some leg stretches against the trig point. Apart from that the hilltop was empty.

Before heading to Raven Howe he continued south as far as the islands in Birthwaite Bay. As he crossed the channel between Ransome Holme and Benson Isle, he spotted *Bobalong*, the dinghy from River's Edge, pulled up on the shingle beach on Ransome Holme.

Joel was casting a line from the beach with a rather clumsy flick of a rod. He looked like he was fly fishing. Maggie was sitting in the bow of the boat, bending over a book. She turned over a page, and pushed some hair behind her ear. He hoped that, just because he had agreed to take them swimming tomorrow, they wouldn't expect him to spend the summer holidays hanging out with them. He would do his bit to keep Aunt Emily happy. But they couldn't expect much more than that. After all, if it was climbing and swimming and playing *Swallows and Amazons* that they wanted, what use was he?

He was about to head east when he noticed a large orange speedboat tied to the jetty on the island on the other side of the channel. Although Benson Isle was the largest island on the lake it was also the least known, having been owned by the same reclusive family since the eighteenth century. Even Jim Rothwell, who knew every inch of the lake, had never stepped foot on it. 'Come to think of it,' Jim had said when Tom asked about it once, 'I don't know anyone who has.' Then, a few months ago, the island had suddenly been sold, but in his many inquisitive flights over it Tom had seen little sign of the new owners, other than some fences appearing. Now, there was the *Invincible* moored up just underneath the *Private: Keep Off* sign. Perhaps the man who owned the fastest boat on the lake, also now owned its biggest and most secluded island. If so, whatever he was up to, he clearly meant business.

Tom pulled *Skylark* into a spiral until he was directly over the famous round house, which most people, speeding by on a tourist launch, only glimpsed through the trees. With every door closed and shutters over the windows, the place looked as deserted as ever. But as he circled around, a figure emerged from the trees. Tom recognized the red-headed woman, who went past the house and disappeared into a concrete outbuilding around the back.

Tom hovered for a few moments, but she didn't reappear. He checked the battery, which showed fifteen per cent remaining. Then he pulled away towards Raven

Howe – the peak where he'd first seen straw-hat man with the laptop.

The flight path to Raven Howe took Tom over a disused slate quarry cut into the hillside. He had flown into it regularly to look at a nest of peregrine falcons, perched high up in the wall of rock. The quarry had always been deserted, but now, parked in the middle of the slate-strewn floor, was a vehicle.

At first sight it looked like an ordinary white van, which would have been unusual enough. But as he circled overhead, Tom could see a plastic ice cream cone moulded into the roof. On the back of the van, in coloured writing, were the words: *Luscious Lakeland – Real Ice Cream, Fresh from the Farm*.

An ice cream van parked up in the abandoned quarry was so out of place that Tom wondered if someone were trying to steal eggs from the falcon's nest. He dropped on to a flat shelf of rock at the top of the cliff and shut down the motors. There were two men in the quarry and Tom recognized them immediately. Standing guard at the entrance was ponytail man. He was cradling something in his hands. Tom felt a jolt as he realized it was a sub-machine gun. He didn't wait this time, but zoomed in and took some photographs.

Then, where the ground fell away into the woods, he saw straw-hat man, now in a blazer and tie, with a clipboard in his hand.

Tom followed his gaze to the road that ran along the eastern shore, where cars like toys crawled along in each direction. Three vehicles were turning on to the track that wound up the hillside to the quarry, all shiny metal and tinted windows, clouds of dust billowing behind. Two black Land Rovers kitted out with spotlights and snorkels accompanied a Bentley SUV, like a pair of body-guards, one at the front, one bringing up the rear. Ponytail man waved the cars into the quarry with his gun. A passenger door of the Bentley opened and a huge bald man in a bright Hawaiian shirt stepped out. Straw-hat man welcomed him with a handshake, and led him to the edge of the quarry. They looked down towards the lake where the *Teal* was making her way through a flotilla of red and blue dinghies.

While they looked at the view, Tom took some more photographs of the strange gathering. They stood around talking for a few more minutes, then the men got into the vehicles and headed back down the hill, the ice cream van bringing up the rear. Tom watched the wisps of dust disperse before starting the motors. As he lifted into the air he glanced down to the lake shore before heading for home. He knew that tourists crossed the world to see sights like this. But something told him these people were not there to enjoy the scenery.

CHAPTER 9

The next morning Tom went to the stone harbour and waited. He watched clouds of midges dancing in columns of light under the trees, and played out the next hour in his mind. He would get the apology done with straight away, show them the river, take them for a swim, get back. The water would be colder than they were expecting, so they wouldn't want to stay long.

When Maggie and Joel arrived, rolled-up towels under their arms, he opened his mouth to offer his half-rehearsed speech, but the dog bounced around his legs, barking ecstatically and Tom had to hold on to a post to stop himself falling.

'Where shall we start?' said Maggie, as she grabbed Archie's collar.

'This is the River Elleray,' said Tom, with a wave of his arm. They looked out over the water. The river was trembling with life. Cream-coloured feathers drifted past and bubbles popped with tiny sighs, as if the energy below the surface were trying to escape.

Maggie closed her eyes and breathed in deeply. 'This place is . . . delicious! And you actually *live* here?'

'Er . . . I do now,' he said, slightly taken aback by her enthusiasm.

'And we've got four whole weeks to explore.'

Joel looked at his watch. 'Actually we've got three weeks, six days and one and a half hours left.'

'Joel, don't start all that.'

Tom studied them, mystified. Both brother and sister had jet-black hair, like their mother's, and dark brown eyes. Maggie was a little older than Tom, and Joel a little younger. Not surprisingly, they both had a hint of a northern accent. But Maggie had a way of speaking that was strangely urgent, almost dramatic.

'Is this your boat?' said Maggie. Tom heard a note of doubt in her voice as she pointed to his scuffed old fibre-glass dinghy, tied up in the harbour, blue paint flaking off her sides.

'That's *Maggot*.' Tom couldn't seem to soften the sharpness in his voice. 'You don't need to worry, she won't sink!'

'*Maggot*,' she repeated. 'I like the name.'

Tom remembered watching her, fascinated, on the top of Brockbarrow. Close up, she was even more intense – she had a kind of pent-up energy that made Tom think of a dog that had been left indoors too long. He knew the feeling. He had to get this over with. He gestured to the steps and held on to the painter while they climbed aboard.

Tom pulled the starter cord and felt the current ease them into the river. With a twist of the throttle the boat found her groove.

'How fast can it go?' asked Joel.

'She,' said Tom.

'What?'

'You always call a boat "she".'

'Sorry. How fast can *she* go?'

'Fast,' said Tom, looking past him to navigate the right-hand bend. 'But we have to stick to the speed limit.'

'So why the big engine?' Joel raised his voice above the growl of the outboard. 'Wouldn't it be more economical to have the right size?'

'I built it myself from three broken ones. It's more power than *Maggot* needs, but it comes in handy occasionally,' said Tom. He couldn't help feeling flattered by Joel's interest, and gave the throttle a sharp twist, to show him what fifty horsepower on a twelve-foot dinghy felt like. The boat lurched, and Maggie was flung along the bench. She laughed, letting the wind blow the hair out of her eyes.

Tom took a deep breath. 'Guys. I . . . er . . . About yesterday when you arrived—'

'Oh, look,' said Joel. '*Podiceps cristatus!*' He pointed to a bird with two candy-striped chicks riding on her back, paddling up stream.

'We call them great crested grebes.'

'They're totally gorgeous,' said Maggie.

They reached the open water and Tom gunned the engine until conversation was impossible and they could taste the spray in their mouths. He would try again on the way back.

When they landed, Joel and Maggie jumped out and helped pull the dinghy on to the gravel beach.

'Thanks,' Tom said, tying the painter to the bleached root of an alder. Guests usually needed telling what to do.

'So you like birds too?' asked Joel, looking at the binoculars hanging round Tom's neck.

'Um. Well. Anything that flies really.'

But Tom had not brought the binoculars for bird spotting, and as soon as the others had begun gingerly wading out into the water, he made his way up the slope behind the beach and began to scan the lake and fell tops for anything suspicious. There was nothing out of the ordinary today. He watched Maggie and Joel splashing each other and laughing at the cold, the dog dashing between them, quivering with excitement. Then, around to his right, through the trees, he spotted a white vehicle in the car park. There was no mistaking the ice cream van, with the plastic ice cream cone, complete with chocolate flake, moulded into the roof, and *Luscious Lakeland – Real Ice Cream, Fresh from the Farm*, in coloured letters on the back. He made his way back to the beach, wondering if he would have time to go and have a look at it, as Maggie and Joel began to tiptoe out of the water, jagged stones on soft feet making them wave their arms about like string puppets.

'See anything from up there?' asked Joel, wrapping a towel around his waist.

'What?' Tom started.

'Any birds?'

'Oh, not really.'

'So what were you looking at?'

'I . . . just some cormorants.'

'Where?'

Tom sighed and handed the other boy the binoculars. He pointed to a rocky island some way down the lake. 'If you look at the dead tree sticking out on that island, you'll usually see a few drying their wings.'

Maggie picked up a pebble and skimmed it over the water, watching it bounce six or seven times, before disappearing with a graceful splash. 'Tom,' she said, 'Joel and I wanted to camp on an island and cook on a fire while we're here. We've never done anything like that.'

'Maggie's reading *Swallows and Amazons*,' said Joel, as if by way of explanation.

'I read all the books years ago,' corrected Maggie, with

a wave of a hand. 'But now we're in the Lake District, I thought I'd see some of the places where they were set.'

Tom looked at his watch, wondering about the ice cream van.

'Where would you recommend, Tom? I bet you know all the islands!'

'One or two,' said Tom. He conjured up a picture in his mind of secluded little Heron Holme, down on the south-west side, with its perfect camping place and sheltered harbour. But he'd always thought of it as his secret. It would probably be too far for them anyway. 'There's only one option for camping at this time of year. It's the second largest of the islands in the middle of the lake, in Birthwaite Bay.'

'When I looked at the map I counted nineteen islands,' said Joel. 'Including some small ones, I admit, but they all had names.'

'The smaller ones are too small,' Tom said. 'Or closed for nesting. The big one with the house, Benson Isle, is private. The one you can camp on is the long, wooded island opposite that.'

'That's the one we went to yesterday evening to fish from,' said Joel. 'Although I didn't catch anything. Any ideas?'

'It's not great for fly fishing,' said Tom. 'You're better off going after perch and pike with a spinner. Especially on the other side of the island.'

Maggie was watching a wooden tourist launch, barbed with selfie sticks, pass by. 'Hold on.' She spun around and met Tom's eyes. He turned away in realization of what he'd said. 'How did you know which side of the island Joel was fishing from last night?'

'Well, I—'

'And how did you know I was fly fishing?' added Joel.

Tom was suddenly furious with himself for being so stupid.

'There's an ice cream van parked over near the big house.' He started towards the path that led around the bay to Dowthwaite House. 'I'll start walking. You can catch me up when you've changed. My treat.'

The van was alone in the desolate car park. Tom's body stiffened with apprehension, as he recognized the profile of ponytail man immediately, now hunched over a laptop.

The man turned and saw Tom staring through the window. He blinked, then slammed the laptop shut, a flash of annoyance in his eyes.

He slid the window open as the others were arriving, and forced a smile. 'What can I get you?'

Maggie pondered the stickers on the window. 'I'd like a Magnum, please.'

The man didn't move. 'Sorry, sold out of those.'

'OK, I'll have a Twister, then, please.'

'Out of those too, I'm afraid.' He scratched the back of his neck impatiently, and as he raised his arm, Tom felt a cold shiver of fear sweep over him. A small, faded tattoo was visible on the back of his wrist. It was the same as the one Tom had seen on the helicopter pilot's wrist: a winged running man – or maybe some sort of angel – with a golden bird under his arm.

'I know,' said Joel reasonably, 'why don't you tell us what you do have, then we can decide?'

'How about a 99?'

He began to fill three cones from the tap, and shot them an apologetic smile, as if he'd suddenly remembered his lines in a play. 'You can have the flakes for nothing, to make up for the lack of choice. I'm a bit new to all this.'

They walked back to the beach, their ice creams dripping on to their hands.

'Urgh,' said Maggie. 'This is the most melty ice cream ever.'

'Well, it is hot today,' said Joel, trying to catch the white liquid that was oozing from his cone in his mouth. 'About twenty-five degrees, I'd say.'

Maggie glanced around the empty car park. 'No, that's not it. There was something odd about that man. He just didn't – you know – look like an ice cream man.'

'Weird,' agreed Joel. 'And how can he have "sold out"? There's no one around.'

'Anyway, what is this place?' asked Maggie.

'It's called Dowthwaite House,' said Tom. 'It's been empty for years but it's been converted into some kind of study centre. I think there's a grand opening happening on Wednesday.'

'Well,' said Joel. 'Somebody *very* important is coming to open it.'

Tom stopped. 'How do you know that?'

Joel pointed to a manhole cover in the ground. 'It's been sealed,' he said, as if it were the most obvious thing in the world.

They all bent down to examine the rusty iron plate, and now Tom could see that several flat pieces of black rubber had recently been stuck on to the ground over the edges of the metal cover.

'When someone very important is about to arrive somewhere,' Joel explained, 'the police go around checking drains and manholes along the route a few days before, in case some terrorist tries to plant a bomb in one of them. Then they seal them with these rubber seals, so they know they haven't been tampered with. But they only do this for real VIPs. We're not talking TV celebrities or football players. I mean proper big guns – prime ministers and presidents and popes, that sort of thing.'

'How do you know about this stuff?' Tom said.

Maggie put her hands on her hips. 'Basically, he's a sponge. He just absorbs stuff. Infuriating when it comes to exams – he barely has to try.'

'I wonder . . .' Joel was looking back at the ice cream van. 'I'm sure Maggie's right about that guy. He's not here to sell ice creams. Maybe he's an undercover policeman – keeping an eye on things before the VIP arrives?'

Tom looked at his watch, suddenly desperate to get home. This was all getting too big. He needed to think. He tossed his remaining ice cream into a bin. 'I think it's time we headed back.'

While *Maggot* bounced through the wavelets, Tom thought how pleased Aunt Emily would be when she heard he'd taken them swimming *and* bought them an ice cream. But then he felt a surge of guilt that he hadn't told them about Heron Holme, which he knew was the best place to camp. The least he could do was let them know about SBS. If they got in the way of Snakey, Noyley and Podge there would be real trouble.

He looked at Maggie, who was dipping her wrist in the water, letting it bounce along the surface like an aerofoil. 'I suppose I should warn you about something.'

'Yes?'

'Watch out for a ski boat called *Stingray*. If you see it, stay away. Some of the local boys think that island – the one you want to camp on – belongs to them.'

'What's it called?' asked Maggie.

'Ransome Holme.'

Maggie's face lit up. 'Is that named after Arthur Ransome?'

Tom shrugged. 'Dunno. Suppose it might be.'

'You do know who I'm talking about, don't you? Arthur Ransome? He wrote the *Swallows and Amazons* books?'

He glared at her, and saw her flinch. 'Of course I do! You know it's not actually the island in the book, though, don't you?' He could hear the harshness in his voice, but he left the words hanging.

Maggie shifted in her seat and the brightness seemed to drain from her face. 'Well never mind,' she said quietly. 'I'm sure it'll be perfect.'

Tom adjusted the choke and pushed *Maggot* towards the river mouth. Aunt Emily was right. Saying sorry was harder than he'd thought.

CHAPTER 10

Tom dropped Maggie and Joel back at the stone harbour, and made sure he kept out of their way for the rest of the day. In the evening he drove to the tree-fringed bay where Jim Rothwell's houseboat creaked and tugged at her mooring. But before he reached the bay, Jim was gliding towards him in *Swallow*, and a few minutes later Tom had anchored *Maggot* and clambered aboard.

'So you saw that beauty I caught on Saturday morning, then?'

Tom thought back to the moment just before *Skylark* had crashed, when he'd clocked Jim holding a decent-sized fish. 'Yeah. Just.'

'I didn't know that machine of yours could go so fast.'

'Neither did I.'

'Keeping out of the way of the big boys, were you?'

'That helicopter? Yeah, kind of.'

'Anyway, six pounds of char. Gave me quite a fight on the way up.' He nodded towards the bamboo poles set on either side of the boat, each with a spherical bell at the tip, and a double line plunging into the depths.

They drifted for a while, the silence broken eventually by a pair of swans flying low over the water, wings creaking.

'So, how come you're not out flying on this fine evening? Something on your mind?'

'Maybe.'

Jim pulled out his pipe and a box of matches and began the mysterious ritual of lighting up. The sight of Jim screwing up his face in concentration as he struck a match and cupped his hand over the bowl always made Tom smile. Jim stretched his legs under the bench. Tom did the same. A scent like fresh-cut hay mixed with autumn bonfires and a hint of fresh toast filled the air. It was the smell of wisdom, Tom thought.

'Out with it then, lad. That Snaith boy been up to no good again?'

'Not really. I've just got a feeling something bad's going on. But I don't know what.'

The sun was sheening on the mercury-smooth water, forcing them to squint. How different everything seemed in daylight. Were there really criminal minds plotting to commit some atrocity in the tranquillity of the English Lake District? What if he had imagined it all? But he hadn't imagined the cruiser, sunk deliberately, with the speedboat looking on. Then there were the three people on the three fell tops; the *Teal* squeezed into the tiny bay, the meeting in the quarry like something out of a spy movie; the suspicious ice cream van; the RAF helicopter; tattoos; police everywhere.

'What have you seen?'

Tom waved an arm towards Raven Howe. 'Not one big thing. Lots of little things. Things no one else would have noticed.'

'A pattern, you mean?'

'Yeah, maybe.'

'Ah! Yes. The extraordinary privilege of flight.'

Tom looked at him blankly.

'You can make all kinds of connections from the air that you can't from the ground. See things you're not meant to see.'

'Yeah, you're right. I suppose that is why I do it.'

'Can you go to the authorities and tell them what you have seen?'

Tom thought about the helicopter pilot with the identical tattoo to ponytail man in the ice cream van; his disbelief, his threat. What if he were mixed up in this too? And what real evidence did he have?

'I don't think so. Not yet.'

'You'll need to join a few dots, then.' Jim tightened the

reels, first on one side, then on the other. 'And I imagine you'll need some help with that. Is there anyone else you can trust?'

'You mean anyone who would believe me?'

'I suppose that *is* what I mean.' Jim chuckled and expelled a blue cloud. They both watched the smoke disperse into the windless air. It was like the vapour trail of a shared memory: the disbelief that had met Tom's theory that his father had not died in the Middle East when his Tornado had been shot down, but was being held hostage by insurgents. The RAF police and Foreign Office had listened with the same pitying expression on their faces. Only Jim had taken the idea seriously.

'Your aunt was excited about some new guests arriving.'

Tom felt himself reddening. He knew he would end up disappointing everyone, because he was such useless company. But what could he do now? He'd never have imagined things could change so fast. They had, though.

'Anyway, you'll need some extra eyes and ears. People who can see what you've seen and tell you you're not mad.' Jim let out a bark of laughter. 'I speak from experience.' He clenched his teeth around his pipe and began to reel in the lines. 'Nothing biting today.'

He began to row back to where Tom had left *Maggot* anchored. The only sound was the rhythmic splash of the blades cutting through water.

'Have you eaten the fish yet?' asked Tom after some time.

'In the fridge. But I'm hoping my good luck will continue for a while longer.'

'Why?'

'Brian Wilkins, the head chef at the Damson Howe Hotel happened to mention a couple of weeks ago that he was after a big char. Said he needed it for someone very special.'

'Did he say who?'

'He did. But he shouldn't have.'

'Why not?'

'Because it's top secret.' He took his pipe out of his mouth and pointed the tip decisively at Tom's chest. 'Look, Tom, it could be that whatever you have seen is something suspicious. On the other hand it might be nothing bad at all – it could all be the police, and so on and so forth, protecting this person. They go to great lengths these days with the threat of terrorism so high. Massive preparation for a visit like this.'

'A visit like what?'

Jim took a puff of his pipe and blew out a jet of smoke to the side of his mouth. 'After opening the new fresh-water study centre at Dowthwaite House on Wednesday, the person I'm speaking about is going to get on board the *Teal* and go for a cruise down to Birthwaite Bay – at three o'clock. There is going to be a reception on the boat involving people from the tourism industry, while they head down the lake. There will be a massive security cordon. No one will get near her. And my fish – if I manage to catch another whopper – is going to be the starter. Can you believe that?'

'Near her? Near who, Jim? Who is it?'

'I mean the *Teal*, of course. No one will get near the *Teal*. Come on, let's get you back. Sounds like you've got work to do.'

Back in the workshop, his mind racing, Tom pulled out his sketch map and grabbed a pencil. He marked the three peaks where he had seen the three people. Jim might be right – it could all have been the security operation getting under way. He had some idea how thorough these things had to be. Berthing the *Teal* in Dowthwaite Bay had obviously been some kind of dry run. Then there were Joel's rubber seals, police RIBs, the Puma helicopter. But could that explain everything? He suddenly wished, with an intensity that was like an electric shock, that he could ask his father. He would be able to join the dots. And then, as it so often did, the image of the burning wreckage of his plane flashed into his mind: twisted metal, black smoke, the open cockpit in the silent desert.

He went to the door and let the fragrant air cool his face. A duck quacked somewhere on the river. He wiped his palms on his T-shirt and went back to the map. He drew a vessel moored at Dowthwaite Bay, and labelled it, '*Teal*'. He then drew three straight lines between the three summits – Raven Howe, Brockbarrow and Rigg Knott – forming a triangle across the end of the lake, its topmost point being Brockbarrow behind his own home.

He wrote 'ICV' and sketched an ice cream van where he'd first seen the vehicle at the quarry. He looked at the position of the doomed cruiser, which he had marked with a cross. Finally, with shaking hands, he drew a line from the jetty at Dowthwaite Bay, through the entrance of the bay out into the open water, the route the *Teal* would have to take at the start of her VIP tour down to Birthwaite Bay.

Tom felt his whole body break into a shudder as he looked at the map with a sudden clarity. The cross, representing the sunken motor cruiser, was at the centre of the triangle. And the line of the *Teal*'s route went right through the cross! The cruiser had been a dummy for the *Teal*, marking her position in full sight of the three peaks: a sitting target. He put his pencil on the desk and put his head in his hands.

What he had drawn in front of him was as innocent-looking as a piece of geography homework. But now he knew what was going on. The orderly lines he had drawn on the map, the neat intersection of the *Teal*, cruiser and trig points, was a sketch of an assassination plot. Someone was planning to send the *Teal*, and whoever was on board, to the bottom of the lake on Wednesday afternoon.

CHAPTER 11

When Maggie and Joel pulled the boat on to the beach on Ransome Holme on Monday afternoon, the first thing they did was remove a pile of beer cans and carrier bags that were scattered around the remnants of a fire.

'Not exactly Treasure Island, is it, Maggie?'

'Nah, I s'pose not.'

'And those were probably not made by Man Friday,' said Joel, pointing to the letters 'SBS', which had been gashed clumsily on a tree.

'You're getting your desert island adventures mixed up there, Joel,' said Maggie, throwing a stick for Archie.

'But at least it's an island. And it's all ours!'

'What is it about you and islands anyway? It's just a piece of rock surrounded by water.'

'Why are you *so* unromantic? An island isn't just a piece of rock. It's an idea, a miniature kingdom, our own little secret world. Anyway, let's stake our patch before someone else does.'

'Tom said something about some boys,' said Joel.

'But he didn't really explain what he meant. He keeps his cards close to his chest, doesn't he?'

'He's a bit shy, I suppose.'

'And I don't ever seem to be able to say the right thing.'

'Laughing when Archie knocks him into puddles probably doesn't help!'

'I tried to say sorry. But he's just . . . prickly.'

'Yeah, but he likes birds and knows about fishing and—'

'But how did he know?' said Maggie, looking back at the little harbour.

'Know what?'

'Where you were fishing. And even what kind of fishing you were doing? Don't you think that's weird?'

'Maybe he climbed up a hill and watched us.'

'Have you seen his limp? I can't see him hiking up hills any time soon.'

'I wonder what happened to him.'

They put up the tent and made a campfire with a circle of stones. In the afternoon sunshine the clearing seemed less secluded than when they'd first seen it. And even on the widest part of the island there was no escape from the steady purr of outboard engines, the distant murmur of tour guides on the steamers and the occasional plastic bump of kayakers in the channels on either side.

Maggie looked around her. 'Come on,' she said, trying to hide the flatness in her voice. 'Let's go and explore. Then we'll light the fire.'

Ransome Holme was shaped like a wedge. The broad southern end was where they had set up camp, and the rest of the island tapered off to a pebbly spit. Opposite the spit, across a narrow channel, was a tiny reed-fringed islet which appeared as if a fragment of the main island had been snapped off and floated away.

'If Ransome Holme is Italy, then that little island is Sicily, being kicked off into the Mediterranean, like a football,' Maggie said.

At the end of the spit was a mound of stunted bushes which had somehow twisted itself into the shape of a bowl, forming a natural shelter facing the lake.

'And this will do as a lookout,' said Joel, stooping into the bushes.

Maggie followed and sat on the mossy ground, leaning her back against the trunk of the rowan that formed the centre of the bush.

'It's a perfect spyhole,' she said, pulling Archie in after her. 'We can sit here in total secrecy and look at the world going past.'

A steamboat glided by, steered by a red-faced man in a stripy blazer, its polished hull slipping through the water with the faintest whisper.

'Look,' said Joel, pointing to a patch of reeds on the shore of the islet.

They watched as a small bird with a long red bill darted into the reeds from the channel, followed by three jet-black chicks.

'*Rallus aquaticus*,' Joel said, as they disappeared from view. The way Joel pronounced Latin words with a slight flourish always made Maggie think of boy wizards casting spells. 'Water rail,' he explained. 'Pretty rare to see one – they're so shy and well disguised.'

They heard the danger before they saw it: a muffled thud of bass over the gargle of a propeller. Then, as if from nowhere, the roar of an engine filled the air, as a massive black ski boat, bristling with tow poles, burst into view.

As the boat came closer, Maggie could see that there were three boys about her own age in it. The one at the wheel was bouncing his hips in a clumsy dance to the techno beat, a can of energy drink in one hand, baseball cap swivelled on his head. He pointed to the channel in front of Maggie and Joel. The engine was cut to idle and the boys seemed to be discussing something.

Maggie grabbed Joel's arm. 'They're playing dares, Joel! He's going to try for the gap.'

Suddenly Joel was up and plunging into the water. 'They'll run aground – and they'll destroy that nest in the process.'

The channel was deeper than it looked and his voice came high-pitched and tight as he waved and shouted, 'Stop! There's a bird nesting here! It's too narrow!'

But the boat was rocketing towards him. Maggie could hear the music over the bubbling violence of the engine. She watched, paralysed, as the bow slapped the water, heard herself screaming at Joel to get out of the way. Now the boy who was driving had seen him. He spun the wheel like a lunatic, turning the boat aside at the last possible moment. Maggie saw the flash of fury on his face, as the boat carved away into its own wash.

She crouched back into the bush holding Archie's collar and gestured to Joel who was now sprawled, half-submerged in the reed bed, to keep still. The engine was idling somewhere nearby and the boys were talking angrily.

'Where's he gone?'

'Wait till I get hold of him!'

'Come on. Let's go and hunt him down.'

CHAPTER 12

Joel crawled out of the reeds and waded across to Maggie, who was shaking.

'It's OK,' said Joel. 'I was planning on jumping out of the way anyway.'

As Maggie and Joel arrived back at the clearing they expected to see the black ski boat moored up in the little bay and they braced themselves for a confrontation. But *Bobalong* was alone.

'Here, Archie, what is it?' called Maggie, as the dog bounded off towards the exposed end of the island again. A few moments later the dog returned with something in his mouth and dropped it at Maggie's feet. It was a white plastic canister, about the size of a hen's egg. Maggie picked it up and prized open the lid. Coiled inside was a scrap of paper with a handwritten note on it.

They've gone to refuel but they will be coming back for you. If you don't want to get hurt, leave the island now. Destroy this note.

They stared at the scrap of paper that was lying on Maggie's palm like a delicate insect, and looked around them. Somewhere through the trees there was the crack of a sail as a yacht tacked out in the channel. But they were alone on the island.

'Maybe,' said Joel, 'one of the other eighteen islands would be better for camping?'

'If you want to chicken out and go home, feel free. I'm staying. And I hope those idiots do come back, so I can tell them what I think of them. Anyway, Tom said this was the only place we could camp.'

They set to work building a fire and kept an almost solemn silence while Joel struck a match. The flames built, then there was the first hiss of sap, followed by the nutty taste of smoke hitting the back of the throat.

Maggie threw the note into flames. 'It must be from Tom. And they must be the boys he warned us about. But how can he have got that message to us without us seeing him?'

'I honestly do not have a clue,' said Joel. 'Pigeons?'

'Anyway, we need to worry about those idiots coming back. The one driving the boat had a certain kind of face.'

'What kind?'

'The dangerous kind.'

Joel, who had begun to shiver in his wet clothes, suddenly started shaking with laughter.

'What's so funny?'

'Well, Mags . . . isn't this the adventure you wanted? Now we've got some real pirates to tackle.'

She punched him on the arm. 'Don't call me that,' she said, 'or I'll make you walk the plank, or something!'

Later, when the sun was sinking behind the trees on the western shore, Maggie was turning some sausages in a pan over the fire, watched intently by Archie, whose fur was steaming in feathered peaks.

'He went in to chase some ducks,' explained Maggie as Joel returned from the lookout. She divided the sausages between two plates with some hunks of buttered bread, and handed one to Joel. 'We should do that tomorrow.'

'What, chase ducks?'

'No, you numpty, go for a swim. I want to swim right round the island.'

'I'll row alongside to protect you,' offered Joel, putting a generous squirt of brown sauce on his sausages. 'You know, in case the pirates come back. Good job they haven't turned up.'

'Yes, but strange too,' said Maggie.

They sat on a log facing the fire, the sausages burning their mouths. The circle of light cast by the fire heightened the gloom. A gentle breeze was knocking some halyards against a metal mast in the channel and a goose honked somewhere. The lake was settling down for the night.

Archie bounded up, his ears pricked. With his nose to the ground he disappeared into the darkness and was back a few moments later with another white canister in his mouth, which he dropped at Maggie's feet. She opened it and laid the note out in her hand, and they peered close to the fire to read it.

They're coming. Ryan Snaith (small, freckles), Samuel Noyland (thin) and Paul Hodgson (not so thin). Leave the island while you still can — they are dangerous.

Just as they had thrown the scrap of paper into the fire, they caught the throb of an engine.

'What shall we do?' said Maggie. 'I'm not going home now.'

'We could climb a tree?'

'They're going to see our boat when they land. That's it!' she said, pulling Joel up by the wrist. 'We need to get into the boat. We'll stay out of their way until they've gone.'

Maggie poured some water on to the fire, grabbed the remains of the sausages and whistled to Archie to follow. They fumbled through the trees to the beach and shoved the boat hard out into the channel before clambering aboard. Taking an oar each, they sculled silently towards the moored yachts.

Out in the open, the first few stars were piercing the deep blue over the crinkled outline of the hills. The lake seemed to glow with a silvery light of its own. The only sound now was the dull throb of the engine, coming closer.

Maggie shuddered, and pushed Archie under a bench. 'Keep low. Make it look like it's empty.' She offered Archie the sausages to keep him quiet.

They sculled through some moored yachts and found a vacant buoy. Maggie grabbed the ring and threaded *Bobalong*'s painter through it. Then they lay down in the bottom of the boat and listened.

The sound of the engine came level with them, and then slowed as the boat turned into the little bay on Ransome Holme. The engine was cut and they heard the bow crunch on the pebbles, a splash as someone stepped into the water, and low voices. There was an argument going on.

'If you'd checked the tank before we left, you idiot, we could have been here ages ago!'

'How was I to know we'd run out of diesel so soon? It's the way you drive, Snakey. Burns more fuel.'

Maggie raised her head over the gunwale.

'Be careful,' whispered Joel.

Three torch beams were moving about in the trees.

The voices were louder now. 'The fire's still warm but they've put water on it, so they can't be far away.'

'Spread out and look.' This was the one in charge. 'Noyley, you go that way, Podge, that way, and I'll stay here in case they come back.'

The three lights separated. After a few minutes of searching the lights came together again. There were whispers, then the sound of a cigarette lighter being struck. Once, twice, and suddenly the island was ablaze with firelight. There was the sound of rushing air. Sparks showered through the branches, as their tent burst into flames and lifted off the ground. The fireball fizzed and hissed for a few moments before the flames turned blue, and then died, leaving pungent fumes in the air, like the smell at the end of a firework display.

Maggie found herself moving in a fog of fury. Nothing she could do seemed fast enough. Her fingers fumbled with the rope. Her hands slipped as she grabbed the wet oars. They pulled the dinghy on to the beach and stumbled over some tree roots. As Maggie and Joel staggered into the clearing, all three torches were turned upon their faces.

Maggie spoke first, her voice breathless. 'You've burnt our tent. What do you think you're doing, you total nutters?'

'Whoops!' came the sarcastic reply. 'Sorry about that. But this is our island. You're trespassing. So get off it, now.' It was the small boy, Snakey, the one who had tried to shoot the channel earlier.

Maggie was conscious of a rumbling growl coming from Archie beside her. Her throat felt tight as she spoke, but she forced the words out, hoping the piece of paper in the canister was not some sort of mistake: 'Trespassing, are we, Ryan Snaith?'

There was a pause. By the glint of surprise in the boy's eyes she knew it was correct. 'Do I know you from somewhere?'

'No. But we know *you*. And you, Samuel Noyland and Paul Hodgson.'

Snakey stepped up to her now and was about to grab her. Before he could, Archie sprang at him and let out a single bark. The boy blinked and stepped backwards. Archie stood firm, snarling deep in his throat. Snakey's mouth twisted in anger, but there was also confusion in his eyes.

'I don't care who you are or how you know about us. You're leaving. Now.'

'Back to friggin' China or wherever they come from, hopefully,' said one of the others.

'Or what?' said Joel.

'Or we'll sink your boat, and you'll have to swim home. Got it?'

'Fine, we'll go,' said Maggie. 'If this were Tahiti, we wouldn't want to be on the same island as you.'

The boys' attention was suddenly caught by something out on the lake and they flicked off their torches. In the darkness beyond the trees, a blue flashing light was moving slowly towards them.

Paul Hodgson swore. 'Police! We need to go, Snakey.'

Snakey hesitated. 'It might just be wardens. They can't do anything, blue lights or no blue lights.' But the boldness had left his voice. They could not hear an engine, only a faint buzzing sound, like a whisk. The trees around them were pulsating and the faces of the boys were picked up in blue, like three startled ghosts.

'Wardens can do enough,' Paul returned. 'My dad will totally kill me if he finds out I took *Stingray* without asking.'

The piercing sound of a siren filled the air and a second blue light was moving around on the other side of the island, towards the harbour.

'That's not wardens. We've got to go. Now!'

The siren stopped and a man's voice came from a loudspeaker somewhere out on the water.

'Attention, attention. This is the police. We are pursuing three juveniles in a powerboat in connection with a suspected boat theft and harassment of lake users. Please report any sightings immediately.'

The other boys were looking at Snakey for a decision. He didn't move. The message was repeated again from the loudspeaker, closer this time. Paul started towards the boat. Then Maggie could hear him splashing about as he pushed the boat away from the beach. As the engine came to life, the two other boys ran after him. They heard the boat accelerate into the blackness and before long the island was silent again.

Maggie was shivering and felt an urge to sit down. 'Now what?'

The blue lights had disappeared without trace. They unloaded the few remaining items from *Bobalong*, grateful that their sleeping bags had not been in the tent when it was destroyed. Then they gathered some sticks, relit the fire and sat on the log where their campsite had been. The fire took hold, and made the night around them seem even darker. They watched the sparks shooting into the circle of sky above the trees. A bat swooped through the smoke.

'Where's Archie?' Maggie said suddenly.

Then, out of the gloom, he appeared, with a white plastic container clenched between his teeth.

This time the note on the paper had been signed.

Sit tight. They won't come back tonight. Tom.
P.S. I'm sorry.

CHAPTER 13

Tom left *Maggot* in the bay next to *Bobalong* and made his way to the clearing, where a thin column of smoke was rising from the remains of a fire and the sun was slanting through the trees on to three motionless bodies on the ground. The smallest of these rose and bent itself around Tom's ankles, barking ecstatically.

'Tom!' said Maggie, squinting at him through bloodshot eyes. 'How . . . ? What time is it?'

'It's OK,' he said. 'I'll explain.' He threw some sticks into the fire, and wafted the embers with a piece of bark. 'It's nearly six. I've brought breakfast.'

'Nice one!' said Joel. He stood up, letting his sleeping bag fall around his ankles.

'Well, I—'

'We're like starving castaways being rescued by a passing ship,' said Maggie. 'I could eat a horse, now I think about it.'

Tom shook his head, smiling to himself at their unflagging cheerfulness, and began to empty a cardboard box packed with food and cooking utensils. A little later the fire was crackling and spitting, and he was handing out fresh white baps stuffed with bacon.

Tom watched Maggie and Joel as they attacked their food, hot fat dripping on to their fingers. He felt good about the night's work. He had freaked out the SBS, and made it up to Maggie and Joel at the same time. Two birds with one stone! But now what? Could he really trust them to help him? Anyone who had made an enemy of Ryan Snaith had to deserve some respect. And now he'd dropped the messages he would have to do some explaining.

He set about making some tea. And while they waited for the kettle to boil, Tom turned his thoughts back to last night, when he'd realized that his secret life was coming to an end . . .

The evening after his discovery in the workshop – the stomach-turning moment of clarity when an array of facts suddenly aligned, like landing lights on a runway – Tom decided to try and have another look over Benson

Isle. The island, with its guard dogs and warning signs, had always intrigued him, but now it was time for a proper nose around. He was on his way there, flying fast and low over the water, when he spotted *Stingray* heading in the same direction. He remembered the conversation he had half-overheard on the last day of school. He had to steady his hands on the controls, as the memory of the locker returned. He climbed higher and watched the three boys erratically head down the lake towards Ransome Holme.

When he saw them trying to shoot the gap, and Joel stupidly trying to stop them, he knew things would turn out badly. If Maggie and Joel's camping trip was about to be ruined, it wasn't really his fault. After all, he told himself, he had warned them. If he helped them now, they'd have to know about *Skylark*, there'd be a big fuss, and everything would be out in the open.

But then, with a rush of shame, he remembered how badly he had behaved when they'd first arrived.

He circled around again, wondering what to do. He saw *Stingray* head off to the fuel depot in Birthwaite Bay, and watched while Joel struggled out of the water and stood on the shore, talking to Maggie. They would be distraught, their day ruined by Snakey, Podge and Sam Noyland. And no one knew what that was like better than he did.

He reached for a notepad and turned *Skylark* home.

'So, let me get this straight,' Maggie was saying now,

clasping a mug of tea on her knees. 'You can actually fly this . . . drone thing . . . up and down the lake and watch what people are doing without them ever knowing. All from your garden shed?'

'Well—'

'Basically you're a spy.'

'I—'

'It explains a lot. That's how you knew where we were on Saturday, what kind of fish Joel was trying to catch, and how you saw the pirates arrive on the island; and sent the little messages to help us.'

'Pirates? Oh, Snakey and his gang. Well, I'm usually keeping my eyes on them. But why were you trying to stop them shoot the gap? You could have got yourself killed.'

'We'd just discovered a water rail nesting on the little island,' Joel explained. 'I thought they might also wreck their boat and kill themselves. But the bird was my main concern, to be honest.'

Maggie laughed at this, although Tom wasn't sure it was intended as a joke.

'What about when it was dark?' asked Maggie.

Tom shrugged. 'Night-vision camera.'

'So presumably it was you who called the police?' said Joel.

Tom hesitated. 'Well, um—'

'Am I right in thinking,' said Maggie, 'that your aunt doesn't know about any of this stuff?'

Tom shrugged.

'How did you keep it so secret?' asked Joel.

'Everyone just assumes that I'm hooked on some computer game or something. The truth is I've never played a computer game in my life.'

'Flying real drones certainly beats computer games,' said Joel brightly. 'Although I guess it means being stuck in that workshop all the time.'

'I don't have much choice about that, do I?' Tom heard the bitterness in his own voice. Maybe this wasn't going to work, after all. He felt a fresh sense of urgency, like something cold on his skin. He'd stayed long enough.

Joel glanced at Tom's stick. 'I'm sorry. I didn't think.'

'Don't worry about it,' said Tom, getting to his feet. 'As a matter of fact, I can fly *Skylark* from anywhere, using a tablet as a mobile base station. But I prefer the workshop.'

'*Skylark*?' repeated Joel. 'Is that—'

'Shh! Listen . . .' Tom cocked his ear to the sky.

'That helicopter's low,' said Maggie. 'Look, it's landing on the big island.'

Across the channel, the treetops in the middle of Benson Isle were bending, as a dark blue helicopter swayed and tilted in descent, and then disappeared from view beneath the canopy.

'Strange,' said Tom.

'Who lives on that island anyway?' said Maggie. 'Joel and I were wondering about exploring there some time.'

'No way,' said Tom. 'The owners are very secretive

and people say there are guard dogs loose in the grounds to stop anyone landing.'

He walked away from the campsite to the water's edge to get a better view. There was a touch of warmth in the air and a bank of cloud had drifted over the valley, covering the peaks and curling over the treetops, giving them a steamy, tropical appearance. He could hear the helicopter engine winding down. It wasn't the Puma he'd nearly collided with three days ago. From the brief glimpse he'd had, he thought it was an Airbus H125, a five-seater popular with private owners. But there had been something unusual about it that he couldn't put his finger on.

Then, from behind one of the yachts moored in the channel, appeared the *Invincible*, the orange speedboat with the triple outboards. Straw-hat man was alone in the boat, and he was making for the jetty on Benson Isle.

Tom felt a cold wave of fear inside, as he looked across the water. There was some secret mischief going on behind that dark curtain of trees. If he could get on his own in *Maggot* somewhere quiet, he could call *Skylark* up from home in minutes and piece the clues together that no one else seemed to notice. This, he told himself, jabbing his stick into the shingle beach as he turned away from the shore, was the one thing he seemed to do well.

CHAPTER 14

Tom went back to the campfire and grabbed his rucksack.

'Where did that dog get to?' Maggie was saying. 'Don't suppose you noticed where Archie went did you, Tom?'

'No. I'm sorry, I've got to go.'

'But you've only just got here.'

'I can't explain now.' He didn't look round. 'I'm sorry,' he said again.

He was making his way to where he'd left *Maggot* when, from somewhere out on the water ahead of him, came the unmistakable fury of a Cobra engine being hammered. Why had he not been watching?

He got to the beach in time to see *Stingray*'s back end slash past a hire boat, leaving it bouncing and rocking like a bath toy, the family inside visibly shaken. The boys were high-fiving each other as the black boat curved away around the headland.

Suddenly the longing for eyes in the sky was all consuming. There was a quiet bay beyond the car ferry, where he could anchor, call up *Skylark* and get to work, without distraction.

Because his bad leg made pushing a boat off a beach almost impossible, he usually left *Maggot* floating in a few inches of water, with a line from each end tied to a tree or root. He waded out to unhitch the stern rope, and noticed a rainbow puddle of petrol fanning out on the water near the propeller shaft. He checked the fuel cap and it was completely loose. Through the trees behind him he could hear Maggie calling for Archie. Across the channel on Benson Isle, the orange speedboat was tied up at the jetty now and he could see the driver walking up the woodchip path that ran into the trees, carrying a briefcase. He clambered into *Maggot* and pulled the starter, but instead of a welcoming gurgle of power, the propeller flicked round a couple of times and then stopped.

'I'm going to kill him this time,' he spat through clenched teeth as he yanked the cord, but there was no sign of combustion. He yanked the cord again, and again, and again, until his fingers stung, but he knew the engine was dead, and that Snakey had messed things up after all.

He hadn't noticed Maggie standing at the bow, watching him.

'What's the matter?' she said.

'Snakey!'

'What?'

'He was here. All of them. They've put water in my fuel tank!'

'Tom, Archie's gone missing. He's not on the island.'

'They must have taken him too. How did they land on the island without us noticing?'

'It must've been when we were all distracted by the helicopter. That's why we didn't hear Archie barking.' She looked over his shoulder to where the hire boat was meandering back towards Birthwaite Bay, still bobbing on the remnant of *Stingray*'s wash, then turned and ran back to the campsite. Tom waded back to the beach with his rucksack, pulled out a nine-inch tablet and slumped on to the pebbles. He opened the screen and typed in a code to activate *Skylark*'s automatic launch and locate function, a feature he had tested a few times but never needed to use before.

It took a few seconds for the computer in the workshop back home to lock on to his position, then the launch icon on the tablet began to blink red, while the flight parameters were calculated.

Behind him he could hear Maggie shouting for Joel to gather their things.

The icon turned orange and the details of the flight path the autopilot would follow to get to Tom appeared on the screen: four and a half miles at forty knots, adjusted for the strong headwind that was blowing up the lake, would give a flight time of six minutes and twenty seconds. He tapped the screen and the launch icon turned green, just as Maggie and Joel arrived back at the beach.

Maggie threw some belongings into *Bobalong*.

'What are you doing?' said Tom.

'We're going after them.'

'It's too late.' Tom didn't look away from the tablet. 'They're long gone, and they're in a fast boat.'

'But they've got Archie!'

'Well, we don't know for sure yet. But—'

'What will they do to him?'

'They'll probably just dump him somewhere and drive off. It's the kind of thing they'd do. But—'

'They're worse than animals, those boys.' Maggie was untying the painter.

'Yeah, pretty much. But I'm trying to tell you that it doesn't matter, because I can find Snakey from here.'

'How?'

'Look.' They followed his gaze past the overhanging branches, where *Skylark* now appeared, a speck of black high in the greying sky, like a long-haul jet on its final descent from some distant land. The drone passed overhead, banked around and settled into a bumpy approach towards them. 'This is *Skylark*.'

'*Spylark*, more like!' Maggie crouched on the pebbles and watched him guardedly.

'Watch the screen.'

Tom deactivated the autopilot and took control, sending the drone spiralling up to four hundred feet. Maggie and Joel bent their heads over the tablet. They could see the whole island, boats passing on either side, their wash spreading out far behind, treetops like lichen, and three people standing on the beach, with their heads bent over a screen.

'Now that's what I call a selfie!' said Joel.

'Come on!' said Maggie. 'Let's follow them. I don't suppose that thing has any weapons attached?'

'Er . . . no,' said Tom. *Who does she think she is*, he thought, *James Bond?*

They watched the screen as Tom circled higher and Benson Isle came into view. At the southern end sat the grand round house, concealed from the lake by enormous Douglas firs and monkey puzzle trees. A path led away from the house over a neat lawn, past a tennis court, to a clearing where the helicopter was parked. The pilot was pacing about on the grass, smoking, but there was no one else around.

'That's weird,' said Joel. 'Can you circle round that chopper again, Tom?'

'What are you doing?' said Maggie. 'We need to look for Archie.'

'Look,' said Joel. 'It's unregistered. No markings at all.'

'I thought there was something odd about it.'

'Very dodgy. Almost certainly some kind of criminals.'

Maggie suddenly grabbed Tom's elbow. 'There they are! They're landing on the other side.'

Stingray, little more than a shadow in the grey light, was hugging the eastern shore of Benson Isle. They watched as the boat nosed on to a jetty, half-hidden by overhanging branches. One of the boys lifted Archie out of the boat and stood him on the planks. The dog watched the boat back away from the island, then headed into the trees and disappeared from sight.

Maggie jumped into *Bobalong* and began to put the oars into the rowlocks.

'I told you, Maggie, you can't land there,' said Tom.

'Try and stop me!' She dug the blades into the water, sending a curtain of water over his feet. Joel shoved the boat off the beach and climbed in at the bow, looking at Tom.

He could see it was going to be useless to argue.

'Wait!' He stumbled into the water again, placed his stick on a bench and passed the tablet to Joel. 'Take control while I get in. This is a mobile base station. I've set it to easy mode for you. You fly the drone by moving the tablet, like you would if you were playing a game on your phone. Tilt it left or right to rotate, front and back to go up and down. The throttle is that little slider. The flight controller – the computer inside the drone – will handle the wind, up to a point. I'll explain as we go.'

Tom gripped the side and hoisted his good leg over

the gunwale, twisted himself round, and flopped on to the bench.

'Explain what?' said Maggie, leaning back into a stroke as *Bobalong* pulled away from the beach.

Tom sat up and looked around. The wind, which had been strengthening all morning, began to gust from different directions, emptying spinnakers like burst balloons and chopping the water into white-tipped wavelets. A bank of clouds with charcoal-grey under-bellies was billowing in from the south. He looked at Maggie, her dark eyes fixed in front of her as she frowned with the effort of each stroke, and at Joel, brain like a computer, head bent over the tablet, having instantly mastered the UAV. This was not how he liked to do things. But Jim Rothwell was right. He couldn't do this on his own.

'Explain what?' Maggie said again.

Tom sighed. 'Everything.' He could feel the cold seeping into the soles of his feet. 'I think this island is being used by some kind of terrorists. And I think they're planning something big.'

Maggie stopped rowing and looked at Tom, blinking.

Joel didn't take his eyes from the screen. 'Look at that man with the ponytail, in front of the house! Isn't that our friendly ice cream man?' He passed the tablet back to Tom. 'You'd better take over. The wind's picking up.'

Tom took *Skylark* higher and banked into a wide circuit of the island. Although the overcast sky would mean the drone would be hard to spot from below, he couldn't take any chances. He could feel it shuddering and buffeting in the wind.

There was a bark from somewhere in the trees.

'And what's all this got to do with Archie and Snakey?' asked Maggie.

'Nothing at all,' said Tom. 'Like I said, it's just their idea of a stupid joke. They know the island's private and we'd have a hard time getting Archie back. But it means that while that guy is on there, you'd have to be crazy to even try.'

'Come on!' Maggie said, looking over her shoulder. 'One more stroke!' They came level with the jetty and, before he could stop her, she was out and running along the planks.

CHAPTER 15

At the end of the jetty, Maggie turned back to the boat. 'Make owl noises to tell me what's going on.'

Tom was looking at her like a stunned fish. 'Maggie, don't be so stupid. It's dangerous.'

'Watch me from *Skylark*. Two hoots for danger, one for all-clear.' She smelt the first drops of rain, as she headed into the wood.

The island felt like another world. Under the trees the air was cool and still. She glanced back and saw the jetty framed by branches, already a long way behind. Ahead the path plunged into darkness. She took a few steps, calling for Archie softly, then paused to listen, but there was nothing. She followed the path until she came to a fork. A twig cracked somewhere in the shadows. She froze, but it was just a squirrel spiralling up a beech tree, startled by her approach.

Then Maggie heard the owl call. Two hoots for danger! She dived into the trees, dropped to the ground and crouched behind a wizened hawthorn, ignoring the brambles clawing at her shins. There were voices and heavy footsteps coming from the direction of the house. Keeping herself pressed as low as she could, she peered through the bush and saw a red-haired woman and the ice cream man with the ponytail, both dressed in over-alls, carrying a large metal box between them. A tall man wearing a straw hat, and carrying a briefcase, followed behind. It was hard to hear more than a few snatches of conversation, but they seemed to be discussing a special guest who was arriving on Wednesday. The guest sounded important, but Maggie didn't recognize the name.

When they had gone, she listened for the all-clear from the jetty, but there was only the sound of the breeze high up in the canopy. Then she realized that Tom and Joel wouldn't be able to see what was happening. They'd spotted the people coming from the house, but once they were under the trees *Skylark* was as blind as she was.

She decided to keep off the path and head through the trees to the other side of the island, where she'd seen Archie dropped off. Keeping low, she pushed her way through the tangle of undergrowth. She heard a rustle of leaves behind her and stopped. Tom had mentioned guard dogs. She twisted her head around slowly and listened. All she could hear was her heart pounding in her ears. She told herself there was nothing to be afraid of. It was probably just a bird. She was on an island in the middle of the most popular lake in England. What was all this stuff about terrorists anyway? Maybe Tom had seen too many James Bond films or something. Or perhaps he was trying to scare Maggie and Joel away, just like Snakey had tried to. She grimaced as she brushed past a mass of waist-high nettles. Her job was to find Archie and she wasn't going until she had.

There was a glare of light ahead where the trees began to thin, and suddenly she was on the edge of a clearing. The blue helicopter they had seen from Ransome Holme was parked in the middle. Now she thought about it, it did look strange without any markings at all, parked silently in this woodland clearing, in the middle of a secluded island on a lake. Whatever these people were doing, they wanted to do it in secret.

The man and woman in overalls were unloading some small steel crates from the helicopter into the box. Maggie couldn't imagine what was inside those crates, but they were handling them as tenderly as newborn kittens. The pilot, a young, twitchy-looking guy with mirror sunglasses was talking to the man in the straw hat by the open door of the helicopter. Maggie couldn't hear much, but it was obvious they were having an argument.

The pilot was flapping his hands around, and talking loudly about a special delivery. The other man listened calmly, responding with the occasional nod or shake of the head. The briefcase lay open on the seat.

There was something about the whole thing that gave Maggie a bad feeling, and she felt the urge to run back to the jetty. But she had to see it out and find Archie. And while she was here, maybe she could find out who these people were and what they were doing. If she could only see what was in the briefcase, perhaps she would know whether Tom was right. She felt sure it would be stuffed full of bundles of cash, as she'd seen in countless movies.

She dropped on to her belly and wriggled her way forward, slow and quiet, as close as she could, until her head was just under a stubby holly bush, right on the edge of the clearing.

It was raining steadily now and a stream of water was running from the leaves on to her hair and down her neck. She waited for her heart to calm down and strained her ears to listen to what they were saying.

'These specialist warheads take a bit of getting hold of,' the pilot was saying. 'We can't simply stockpile them before you have firm orders. We acquire to order. What more do you want, Mr C?'

'What I want is some trust.' The tall man in the straw hat spoke quietly, and pronounced every syllable crisply. He reminded Maggie of Mr Baker, the head teacher at her school. He never raised his voice, but everyone quaked when he spoke. 'Surely you people must realize that this whole business is built on one person trusting another.' He pulled something from the briefcase and offered it to the pilot. 'You see, here's your payment, on delivery, as promised.' Maggie's pulse raced for a moment, but it was just an ordinary brown envelope. 'I already have orders being placed for this product, even ahead of the show. But if production is slowed down by an unreliable supplier . . . there will be *repercussions*.'

The pilot took the envelope. 'Understood, Mr C. And what shall I say to the chief?'

'Tell your boss to watch the show from Astrum Seven, at 15.03. Then he'll see for himself. It's going to be *spectacular*.'

'Where, Mr C?'

'Routine. Victor. Hoped.'

The pilot climbed into the cockpit and shut the door. Maggie watched the others step away from the aircraft, as the blades began to rotate. She pressed herself flat against the earth and hoped no one would look her way. Then, to her horror, Archie burst into the clearing. He'd come from the path that led to the house, and stood, panting, looking at the helicopter. Maggie watched, hardly breathing, wondering what to do. They hadn't seen him, but as soon as they turned to go back to the house they would. Maggie dreaded to imagine what kind of *repercussions* there would be when they did.

The rotors were singing through the air now, and Archie was rooted to the spot, sniffing the wind, like he would from a car window. She watched helplessly as the engine wound itself up to take-off speed. Up a tone, and up again. Twigs and leaves and dirt were blowing everywhere, and the whole island seemed to shake.

She felt for a stick in the undergrowth, found one, and grabbed it. Then the helicopter lifted from the ground, and as the people in the clearing put their hands over their eyes to shield them from the dust, she threw the stick to Archie. He looked up as the stick landed at his feet, saw Maggie's head under the bush, picked up the stick in his teeth and bolted to her, his tail wagging madly. She grabbed him by the collar, pulled herself, shaking, from the bushes and ran.

CHAPTER 16

While Tom and Joel had been hunched over the tablet trying to see what Maggie was doing, and taking photos of anything they could see on the island, *Bobalong* had drifted several boat-lengths away from the jetty. By the time they had seen the terrorists head back towards the house from the clearing, Maggie was pelting along the wooden boards, Archie at her heels. But now she had nowhere to go.

Tom thought he'd be a quicker rower, so he handed the tablet back to Joel, and picked up the oars.

He glanced over his shoulder, straining against the wind.

Maggie was like a Brimstone missile, coming out of those trees. She charged along the jetty, and, without a single twitch, sprang off the end like an Olympic diver, arced through the air and hit the surface in front of the boat. Archie skidded along the jetty, and then plunged in after her. When Maggie reappeared, spluttering but alert, she had swum under the boat and was hidden from view from the island. To Tom's relief no one appeared on the jetty. Somehow, Maggie had done the whole thing without being seen.

Tom pulled hard on the oars for a few strokes, and once they were well away from Benson Isle again, Maggie heaved herself into the boat, and lay on the bottom, panting and laughing with relief.

'*Routine. Victor. Hoped*,' she said. '*Routine. Victor. Hoped.*'

'What's that?' said Tom.

'*Routine. Vic—*'

'Tom!' Joel interrupted, scowling at the screen. 'I've lost control of *Skylark*. I can just see water.'

Tom felt a shadow passing overhead, and looked up. It was *Skylark,* dipping in the wind, a hundred feet over their heads.

'Steady, Joel. Keep her facing into the wind. Try and land somewhere.'

Tom looked over his shoulder as the drone lost height over the channel between the two islands. He watched it slow almost to a stall, as Joel tried to bring it down on the beach at Ransome Holme, but a sudden squall of wind flipped it on to its back and it plummeted down.

Joel looked confused. 'The picture's gone black. I can't see a thing.'

When *Skylark* hit the water Tom found himself thinking it was almost graceful, like the silken splash of a cormorant when it dives.

A few minutes later, he pulled *Skylark* from the lake and examined it, while it dripped into the boat like a freshly caught fish.

'I'm really sorry,' said Joel. 'Will it be ruined?'

'I don't know yet,' said Tom. 'It couldn't be helped. The memory card should be fine, and that's what matters. Those photos we just took are our only real evidence.'

They went back to Ransome Holme to collect *Maggot* and tied the painter to *Bobalong*'s stern as a tow rope. They hoisted the sails and the steady breeze blowing up the lake pushed them homewards in a few long tacks, *Maggot* surfing the wash behind.

'You're dead right about those people, Tom,' Maggie said, when she had caught her breath. 'I don't know what they're up to, but it's bad. Thanks to your owl call I hid behind some bushes, but I'm sure if I'd been a second later, I would have been captured. I could almost smell the evil on that island. It was like—'

'Maggie!' Joel snapped his head round at his sister. 'Just tell us the facts.'

Maggie scowled at him. While Tom steered them home, the water creaming under the bow, she told them what she had seen and heard on the island.

'"Watch the show from Astrum Seven"?' Joel mused.

'No idea what it means,' said Maggie. 'A TV channel, maybe?'

'Could be,' said Joel. 'Or a satellite, perhaps? Interesting.'

'Did you pick anything up about a VIP arriving?'

'Now I think about it, I did hear them talking about a "special guest" who was arriving on Wednesday.'

'Wednesday?' Tom started, jerking the tiller, so *Bobalong* lost the wind and quivered and flapped for a few alarming moments. 'Who, Maggie?' he said, straightening the boat and tightening the sail. 'Did they say who it was?'

'Yes, but it's no one really famous,' said Maggie. She flicked her hair dismissively. Tom could tell she was disappointed. 'It's just some guy called the Duke of Lancaster.'

Back at Cedar Holme, Maggie went to change into some dry clothes while Tom retrieved the memory card from *Skylark*, and they gathered around a table in the workshop for what Maggie insisted on calling a 'council of war'. Aunt Emily, visibly thrilled to see them all together, brought in a tray of freshly baked cheese scones, along with a huge pan of pea and ham soup, butter, cheese, crisps, a tin of flapjack and a bottle of lemonade. As she set them on the table, she gave Tom an encouraging smile.

Tom sat back on a fold-up chair and watched the two

siblings as they set into the food gratefully, and went over the day's events. Was it just the way they were wired, or did they find the whole thing amusing and exciting, like it was all some great adventure laid on for their holidays? And he began to wonder whether he was right to take them into his confidence, after all.

'When I saw Archie shoot into the clearing, I thought that was game over,' Maggie said, grabbing a fistful of crisps. 'If they'd spotted me then, they would have caught me for sure.'

'And probably put you in that concrete bunker and tortured you for weeks on end,' said Joel, dipping a generously buttered cheese scone in his soup.

'Yeah,' laughed Maggie, 'and I would have offered them my brave little brother as a ransom, without a moment's hesitation!'

Tom stretched out his leg, which was aching with the damp. 'At least you were able to hear what you did when you were hiding in the trees. It's confirmed everything I'd already worked out on my own. With that, and the pictures I took from *Skylark*, I've got all the proof I need now.'

Maggie put down her mug of soup and looked at him, suddenly serious. 'You mean *we've* got the proof *we* need, don't you, Tom?'

'Well, I—'

'If you want us to help you, you're going to have to trust us. Especially as I nearly got captured by those terrorists!'

Their eyes locked for a moment and he knew she could see right through him. He felt his cheeks reddening and wondered what she *really* thought of him: limping, irritable, electronic gadgets instead of friends. He looked away and stared at the tin Aunt Emily had brought the flapjack in: a commemorative Diamond Jubilee tin that had originally held shortbread. He pictured Maggie bolting along the jetty and diving into the lake and found himself smiling back at her in amazement. When she'd landed on the island, and asked him to look out for danger from *Skylark* she had trusted him completely. Now it was time for him to do the same.

'OK, then.' He shrugged, but inside he felt as if a tightly coiled spring was being released. 'We'd better get to work!' He picked a chunk of flapjack from the tin. Then, one step at a time, he filled them in on everything he had seen, and explained his theory that what Maggie had overheard on Benson Isle was part of a terrorist plot to send the *Teal* and the Duke of Lancaster – whoever he was – to the bottom of the lake on Wednesday afternoon.

'Unbelievable,' said Maggie, shaking her head. 'You worked all this out with that little *Spylark* drone thing!'

'So how do you think this attack is going to happen?' said Joel.

'15.03 must be the time of the attack. Three minutes after leaving the jetty in Dowthwaite Bay is all it would take for the *Teal* to be in exactly the right place.'

'Maggie!' said Joel, grabbing Maggie's arm. 'What

was it you were saying in the boat, just before I crashed *Skylark* in the lake?'

'Oh, I'd almost forgotten,' said Maggie. She paused for a moment, eyes wide with concentration. '*Routine. Victor. Hoped.* That's what the straw-hat guy – Mr C – said when the pilot asked, "where?"'

'I think that might be a digital address,' said Joel. 'Anyone in the world can locate any three-by-three-metre square of space, if they know the three-word combination.'

Tom took his laptop from a workbench and tapped the words into a map. 'I knew it! That's the very spot I had worked out from mapping the triangle set by the three trig points, and where they sank that old cruiser, *Clementine.*'

'The dummy run for the *Teal*?' Joel was now sitting with his feet on the table, working his way through a handful of crisps.

'Exactly. So, this is what I think is going to happen. After opening the new freshwater study centre at Dowthwaite House, the duke will board the waiting *Teal* and head straight out for the cruise. As the *Teal* turns out of Dowthwaite Bay she'll be in the line of sight of the three trig points, and from there they will attack.'

'Why can't they just attack from the lake?' asked Maggie.

'Because the place will be crawling with people protecting the *Teal*,' said Tom. 'I think they will each fire some sort of weapon at the same time, from the three trig points.'

'But why from three different places?'

'I guess it gives them three chances of hitting the target.'

Aunt Emily tapped on the metal doors, and came in with a tray of hot chocolate.

'Thanks,' said Maggie. 'Oh, Mrs Hopkins . . . er . . . Emily? I don't suppose you've heard of the Duke of Lancaster, by any chance?'

'Of course I have, dear.' She bent over and tapped the flapjack tin. 'The Duke of Lancaster is Her Majesty the Queen! They are one and the same.'

CHAPTER 17

No one spoke as Aunt Emily's footsteps faded. A pair of magpies chuckled in the cedars.

Joel puffed out his cheeks. 'Like I said. Not TV presenters and football players.'

'Wow.' Maggie picked up the tin. On the Union Jack lid was a smiling portrait of the Queen in a cream-coloured hat with the words: *Celebrating Sixty Glorious Years: 1952-2012* around it. 'Who are these people anyway? We need to find out.'

'Tom,' said Joel, 'what are those numbers on the side of boats?'

'Every powered vessel on the lake has to be registered

with the National Park Authority and display a five-figure number at all times. I didn't take a note of the *Invincible*'s number, I'm afraid. But how would it help anyway?'

Joel reached for the laptop. 'I did. It's 64431. All we have to do is hack into the right database and find the relevant file. Pleasure-boat numbers are hardly national security stuff.'

Joel tapped away at the computer, and by the time Tom had cleared the lunch things away, he had what he was looking for.

'*Boat name:* Invincible. *Model: Vulcan. Manufacturer: Marlin Sport Boats. Engines: Tohatsu Four-Stroke; Two Hundred Horsepower; three.*'

'That's the one!' said Tom. 'Who would need that sort of power?'

'Well,' said Joel, 'you said yourself it comes in handy sometimes.'

'Yes, but six hundred horsepower on a lake with a ten mile an hour speed limit?'

'Here's our Mr C, I think. *Owner: Mr Rufus Clay.* Ah, pity, there's no local address, just a PO box in . . . the Cayman Islands.'

'It's not enough,' said Tom. 'What about the ice cream van? Could that be a clue as well?'

'One specializing in horrible ice cream,' said Maggie.

'Good call,' said Joel. 'Let's try good old Google.' He tapped away for a few minutes. 'Here we go. Not just an ice cream van, but an ice cream company. The Luscious

Lakeland Ice Cream Company. Registered as a new business in February last year. Directors: Rufus E. Clay, Mike J. McCain and Dr Victoria Juniper. Now let's see.' He tapped something into the search engine, and a few moments later brought up the face of ponytail man, unmistakable even without a ponytail, wearing full khaki combat gear, and then the red-haired woman, whose picture showed her in an academic gown receiving a PhD in Aeronautical Engineering. 'Mr McCain also has an address in the Cayman Islands. But now the ice cream company is registered in . . . Hollowdale, Cumbria, UK.'

'Hollowdale?' said Maggie

'It's north of here. Middle of nowhere, really,' said Tom. 'Not an obvious choice for an ice cream factory, but it would be a great place for a terrorist HQ.'

'I can't find anything else on Rufus Clay. It can't be his real name, I guess.'

'May I?' asked Maggie, picking up the laptop. 'It's probably too obvious but . . .' She tapped 'Rufus Clay' into Google Images.

'Why didn't I think of that?' said Joel, shrugging.

'Because,' said Maggie, 'you have a certain kind of brain. And I have another.' They hunched together to look at the hotchpotch of faces and pictures brought up by the search engine: a newborn baby and a happy mother in hospital; an old man, with a long beard sitting on a stool playing a banjo surrounded by hay bales; a teenage boy posing by a lamp post with a skateboard. Joel clicked to a second page, to be greeted by banjo man again, after which the images became more and more random.

'There!' said Maggie, pointing to a photograph of a sports team. She indicated a tall young man on the second row, almost a head above the men on either side. 'It's him,' she whispered.

'Are you sure?' said Tom. He leant close to look at the grainy face staring back at him.

'Look – that face, light hair, glasses. I'd remember him anywhere.'

'Who are those people?' said Tom.

But when Joel clicked on the image itself to try and get to a web page, an error message came up.

'It's an orphan: an image somehow floating around the internet, whose original page had been removed. What can we get from the picture itself?'

It was a picture of a football team, arms folded, front row sitting, back row standing behind, goalie all in black, holding a ball in gloved hands.

Maggie nudged Joel. 'Go on, Sherlock, now's your chance.'

Joel shrugged, then took the laptop and stared at the picture.

After almost a minute he let out a long breath. 'Our friend Rufus Clay is a retired soldier. This is an army unit of some kind. Look at the way every sock is perfectly pulled up, all the boots shiny and clean. They're in a hot part of the world. Look at the bright light, the way they are squinting at the camera, their suntans, the dust at their feet – not grass. And that vehicle in the background. Looks like a rocket launcher. Satellite dish. High tech. I'm guessing they're some sort of engineers.'

'Impressive,' said Tom. And he meant it.

'Hang on,' said Joel, holding his hand up. 'There's a symbol on their shirts. It's a bit grainy.'

Maggie bent over the screen and then gasped. 'It's that naked man. The ice cream man had that tattooed on to his wrist.'

'Yes,' said Tom. 'I saw it too. It's a man with some sort of golden bird under his arm.'

'I didn't see the tattoo,' said Joel, 'but I think I know what it is. It's not a naked man, Maggie. It's a Roman god. Mercury, the winged messenger. And that will be the clue to who these men are. Hold on . . . ' He tapped something into the search engine. 'Yes, here we are . . . it's the emblem of the Royal Signals. Which means,' he said with a note of triumph, 'that our Mr Clay is an expert in electronic warfare.'

Maggie stood up. 'Right. We've got photos and we've got a name. Now we go to the police.'

'But what about the memory card?' said Joel. 'We don't know if it survived getting wet yet.'

'I think it will be OK,' said Tom. 'Solid state storage is hard to destroy. I've put it on the kitchen windowsill to dry in the sun. And you're right, Maggie. We do need to report this. The problem is working out who we can trust.'

'How do you mean?' said Maggie.

'When I saw the tattoo on the ice cream man, it was the second time I'd seen it in the space of a week.'

'Who else did you see it on?'

Before Tom could reply, there was a loud crash on the roof above them, followed by the squawk and fluttering of a startled bird.

'Listen!' said Maggie. The sound of a motorboat was receding into the distance.

Joel ran outside and brought back a jagged piece of slate with a crude skull and crossbones scratched on to one side. Underneath a rubber band was a piece of paper, which Joel unfolded.

If you want it back, come and get it.
SBS.

'SBS?' said Maggie. 'We saw those letters carved on a tree on the island.'

'Special Boat Squad,' said Tom. 'It's what Snakey's lot call themselves. But come and get what? What have they taken? Not *Maggot*?'

'No,' said Joel. 'It . . . she's still there in the harbour.'

'Strange.'

Outside they could hear the magpies flapping and fussing as they settled back into their nest.

'Could Snakey be mixed up with Rufus Clay?' asked Maggie.

'Snakey's an idiot, but he's no terrorist. He wouldn't have the guts, for one thing. No, whatever they've taken, this is just the usual bullying to keep us off their island.

But right now we've got more important things to think about. Let's see if that memory card is dry yet.'

As Tom walked out of the workshop, he thought about going to the police. Of course, now they knew how serious things were, they had no choice. He would simply give the memory card to the police and let them take it from there. On the other hand, it might be the most dangerous thing they could do. Rufus Clay clearly had some powerful friends and if people like the RAF Puma pilot, who were supposed to be guarding the Queen, were involved in his plot, by tipping them off about what he had discovered, Tom would be putting himself and everyone connected to him in danger.

He could hear the whirr of the lawnmower some-where as it worked its way around the garden. The sky had cleared completely and warm sunlight bathed the southern side of the house.

Tom reached his arm through the open window to where he had left the memory card next to a pot of parsley, but there was nothing there and the plant was lying on its side, a handful of soil scattered over the worktop. He put his head through the window and searched the sill and the surrounding sideboards. He hunted around below the window. He then went inside the house and searched the kitchen itself: in the sink, on the floor, under the cupboards. His throat tightening, he went to find Aunt Emily, who was doing some ironing in the utility room.

'Aunt Emily, I don't suppose you've seen a small piece

of shiny metal, about the size of a postage stamp?' he said desperately.

'No, dear, I haven't. Is it important?'

Tom hesitated. For a few seconds the only sound was the hiss of the steam iron as he went over in his mind the fact that the small piece of metal he was looking for contained the key proof for a terrorist attack on the Queen of the United Kingdom, an attack that was less than twenty-four hours away, and whose prevention, he now understood with a prickle of alarm, solely rested on him and his friends.

'Oh, no, it's nothing really.'

CHAPTER 18

A few moments later the three of them stood on the lawn outside the kitchen window, eyes like spooked deer.

'But how on earth did Snakey happen to look on the windowsill?' said Maggie at last.

The whirr of the lawnmower was growing stronger.

Tom shrugged. 'I guess they must have been sneaking around looking for something to take.'

The machine rounded the corner of the house and crossed the lawn in front of them. They watched it silently as it returned to its recharging point, like a well-trained animal. They heard the motor power down and then a click as the contacts were engaged.

'Pity,' said Joel at last.

'On to Plan B, then,' said Maggie. 'Whatever that is.'

Despite having no solid evidence to give them, they did phone the police. Tom decided that they should call the Crimestoppers number and give the information anonymously. Maggie did the talking, with the others listening, and relayed everything they knew in great detail. The man at the other end had a Birmingham accent and Tom imagined him in some huge call centre somewhere in the Midlands. He took everything down with the same matter-of-fact tone that he would if they were reporting a missing cat, or some noisy neighbours. He needed the name of the lake spelling out for him, and Maggie had to explain about the three fell tops and the *Teal* and the lines intersecting where the cruiser had sunk three times before he understood what she was saying.

'I'm just going to put you on hold for a second and see if I can find any information about this incident on file, OK?'

They were hunched around Maggie's phone and some cheery pop music came from the speaker while they waited. Tom thought again about what the Puma pilot had said. He'd accused Tom of 'nosing around a sector under surveillance'. Beneath the air force jargon was a simple and clear message: *mind your own business, we've got it sorted.*

The voice came on the phone again. 'I'm sorry to keep you waiting. We have no record of a boat called *Clementine* being reported missing, so I can't give you a crime number at this point. But I can confirm that the event on Wednesday is being covered by a number of security services, so I suggest that if any criminal activity were to take place surrounding the event they would know about it already. However I have logged the information you've provided. Is there anything else I can help you with today?'

Tom spent the rest of the afternoon in his workshop, repairing the morning's damage. *Skylark*, which had suffered a broken aileron and an electronic failure from the crash-landing in the lake, needed a bit of soldering and a new circuit board. *Maggot*'s waterlogged outboard was another matter, but Tom shut the doors, put his overalls on, laid out his tools, and settled down to the task, glad to be doing something with his hands. He made a start by siphoning the fuel tank. He was gripping the rubber hose between his teeth when the doors opened and Maggie walked in, followed by Archie, who pressed his body against Tom's leg. Unbalanced, he toppled against the engine stand, sending engine parts crashing to the floor, and the hose spurting fuel on to his overalls.

'Archie, sit down!' Maggie scolded.

Flustered, Tom began to pick up the engine parts.

Maggie bent down to help, laughing. 'I'm sorry about

Archie. He does really seem to like you.'

Tom could feel the dog sniffing his overalls where the fuel had spilt, and he found his hand running over his head between the ears, where the fur felt soft and creamy. 'He's got a strange way of showing it!'

'What were you doing with that pipe in your mouth anyway? Drinking it?'

He sighed audibly. 'Siphoning the water out.'

'I'll leave you to it. Sorry for bothering you.' She turned to go, when the events of the last twenty-four hours came flooding back to him. She had been intimidated by Snakey, nearly lost her dog, almost been caught by ruthless criminals on Benson Isle, and he hadn't heard a word of complaint.

'The water is heavier so it settles on the bottom,' he explained gruffly. 'You can then siphon it out, just using gravity.'

'Can I do anything to help?'

'Not really.' He began to loosen a spark plug with a spanner. 'Well, I guess we need to work out what to do now the memory card's gone. That's what I was thinking about.'

'Me too. What about getting the memory card back?'

'How?'

'Go to Snakey's house and make him give it to us?'

'What? And tell him we'll burn his house down unless he gives it back?' Tom found himself smiling at the idea.

'Well, that would be fair, after what he did to our tent!' She laughed. 'Or we could search his place and find it ourselves. Don't you have a drone or something that can do it?'

'Well, there's *Gnat*, I suppose, but how would we—'

'*Gnat*?'

'A micro-drone. But how would we know where—'

'A *micro-drone*?' Tom could feel her looking at him with those laser eyes. 'You've *got* to show me this!'

Tom put the spanner down and picked up his walking stick, which was resting on the side of the workbench. He unscrewed the handle and brought out of it a metal cylinder, about the size of two corks put end to end. He squeezed a lever on the side of the cylinder and a pair of rotor blades sprung into position with a click. He handed it to Maggie, who cradled it in open palms. 'This is *Gnat*.'

He twisted the detached end of the stick to reveal a tiny control panel and screen, which he now held like a small game controller. He pressed a button and the machine whirred to life in Maggie's hands like a fragile bird and lifted into the air, ruffling her hair with the breeze of the rotors.

'It has a little extendable hook on the bottom for picking things up. It's only got a payload capacity of fifty grams, but it's enough to make the occasional item of homework mysteriously disappear from certain people's school bags! The batteries are charged by kinetic energy. The movement of the stick.'

'Love it! But why are you stealing homework, Tom?'

'Revenge. Sometimes if you want to fight back, you have to be creative.'

She nodded. 'Yes, you do! It's like something out of a spy movie.'

'It does the job,' said Tom, plucking it from the space between them and folding the rotor blades up. But inside he was smiling. He slotted *Gnat* into the tube again. 'I don't think we'll be able to find the memory card, though. Snakey will have hidden it.'

'So what should we do?'

'I think,' said Tom, screwing the handle back on to his stick, 'that it's time we paid a visit to Jim Rothwell. Apart from anything else, he makes the best cakes you've ever tasted.'

CHAPTER 19

Later that evening, as the breeze was dying, they pulled into the quiet bay where Jim Rothwell's houseboat, *Matilda*, was berthed. The old wooden boat, with her tarred hull and lime-washed decks, blended into the surroundings as easily as the twisted alders that fringed the shore. Tom killed the engine and let *Maggot* drift into the rope fender. They caught the smell of baking coming from inside, and Tom rapped on the galley window, before climbing aboard.

After quick introductions Maggie and Joel were squashed together on a bench on one side of the table, while Jim got to work in the galley. Tom paced about in the living area, absently looking at the framed photos that lined the walls.

'Food first, talk second,' Jim had replied when Tom told him they needed his advice about an urgent matter. He brought out a bottle of home-made elderflower cordial and some fizzy water, and began chopping potatoes, while he asked Maggie and Joel about themselves. Tom looked on, amazed at how effortlessly Jim could get to know new people. Their mum was born in China, but had come to the UK to study. Their parents met at university. Maggie and Joel had both been born in Manchester, where their father worked as a vet. Joel had been homeschooled by his mum for a few years. Jim didn't ask why. They both spoke fluent Mandarin Chinese.

While they talked, the hot smell of fat leaked into the air from a small electric fryer. Jim plunged the chips into the fat with a hiss. Then he brought out a long grey fish with a pink underbelly.

He took a sharp knife and proceeded to fillet the fish with practised precision.

'Jim, we need to—'

'It's OK, Tom.' Jim raised a calming hand. 'No one thinks well on an empty stomach. You agree, don't you, boy?' he added, rubbing Archie's muzzle.

Tom fiddled with his untouched glass.

Jim placed the fillets in a frying pan, tearing up a couple of bay leaves and scattering them on the fish and the cabin filled with an aroma that made their mouths water.

'Now,' Jim said, raising his voice above the sizzling and spitting coming from the pan. 'These will only take a couple of minutes and then we'll be ready for char and chips, *chez Matilda!*'

As they ate the pearly flesh and burnt their mouths on the chips, Tom filled Jim in on everything they knew, with the others adding bits and pieces as they remembered them. As always, instead of telling him the answers, Jim gave him space to think.

And now everything seemed terrifyingly clear.

Tom pushed his plate away and looked at the others. 'If you think about it logically, we only have one option tomorrow.'

'I told you you'd think better having eaten,' said Jim. He looked at Maggie. 'You see, while we were chattering away, Tom's got it all worked out!'

'It's clear the police aren't interested,' Tom continued. 'And it's not surprising why: an overheard conversation; a theory about missiles launched from mountaintops coordinated (maybe) by an ice cream van! It sounds ridiculous. No one would ever take that seriously without some proof.'

'And now there's no time to get the memory card back from Snakey,' said Maggie.

Joel wiped the oil from his plate with a piece of bread. 'And we're not sure we can trust the authorities anyway,' he said, 'because your helicopter pilot has the same Mercury tattoo as our friendly ice cream man, Mike McCain. A small, but possibly significant, detail.'

'We can't sit back and do nothing,' said Maggie.

'No. We can't do nothing,' said Tom. 'If we can't convince the police, we need to *be* the police, and prevent the attack ourselves.'

'Yes,' said Joel, rather too matter-of-factly, Tom thought, given the enormity of what this was going to involve.

Maggie picked up the last chip with her fingers, mopped up some salt with it, and crunched it. 'Well?'

'Remember when you were on Ransome Holme and you thought the island was surrounded by police boats?'

Joel turned his head slowly to face him in a way that reminded Tom of the rotating turret of a tank, swivelling his neck a hundred and eighty degrees, while keeping the rest of his body completely still. 'That was you? I should have guessed!'

'Just a couple of adapted multi-rotors with blue lights.'

'But the voice wasn't yours.'

'Digital voice filter.'

'Very cool,' said Joel.

'So we tell them that they're surrounded, and the game's up?' said Maggie.

'Exactly. Even though we don't know how the attack is going to work in detail, we know enough to make sure we can be at the right place at the right time. As soon as the men appear on the trig points we can buzz them simultaneously using *Skylark* and two hexacopters.'

'What about SBS?' added Maggie. 'What if that lot

show up and get in the way?'

Tom turned to Jim. 'Jim, would you be happy to row about in *Swallow* as an extra pair of eyes and ears? We'll have to coordinate things from the workshop.'

Jim wiped his mouth on a napkin and reached for his pipe. Tom knew what this meant and he kept quiet. Maggie was looking at the snapshots of Jim's life in the framed photographs on the wall. There was a picture of Jim standing in a boat, looking up at the camera, holding a huge pike by the gills. It was one Tom had taken when he was first testing *Skylark*. Next to it was a picture of a younger Jim, suntanned, surrounded by African children, in front of a rough wooden building. Then there was one of a bride and groom – Jim standing next to a young woman with a kind, open smile and long blonde hair, and they were beaming at the camera. Tom saw Maggie glance at Jim's left hand, as he raised the lighted match to his pipe, head bowed in concentration. He still wore his wedding ring after all this time.

He puffed out a cloud of blue smoke. 'I'm afraid I can't do that, Tom. You see I'm going to be on the *Teal* myself tomorrow.'

Tom heard himself whisper: 'No, Jim.'

Jim held up his palm again. 'Tom, do you remember I told you that Brian Wilkins, the head chef at the Damson Howe Hotel, was after a big char, like the one we've just eaten? Well, fortunately I caught another whopper. He wants it for the very special lunch they are going to serve the very special guest, whom you now all know is to be

Her Majesty the Queen. They want to showcase some local delicacies, you see. Now, let me see if I can remember what he said. There's going to be my char, poached with a wood sorrel sauce, followed by a leg of local Herdwick lamb, slow roasted, served with Lyth Valley damson sauce. And Kendal Mint Cake ice cream with Grasmere Gingerbread for pudding.' He sucked his cheeks in and then expelled a jet of smoke towards the ceiling.

The others found themselves watching the thinning cloud swirl about against the wood panelling of the cabin, as if somehow the smoke carried Jim's thoughts.

'But that led to an invitation. They need to be able to wheel out a crusty old dinosaur with a bit of local knowledge. As the *Teal* swings out of the bay, I'll be standing on the port side giving a little talk about the lake, its history, industry, flora and fauna and so on and so forth. So, by a remarkable coincidence, as the clock strikes three minutes past three, I will be the human being in closest physical proximity to Her Majesty. If all else fails, I'll be there to stand in her path.'

Tom gave a start, knocking over an empty glass. 'But, Jim, you won't be able to stand in the path of these people. I saw the cruiser sink in seconds. That's what they're going to do to the *Teal*. Everyone on the boat is going to die.'

'We'll see.'

Joel was opening and shutting his mouth. 'Wow,' he said at last. 'Do you love the Queen that much? I'm sure she's a great woman, and she's – well, she's the Queen –

but I can't imagine feeling that way about someone I don't even know.'

'Oh!' Jim waved his hand at Joel as if he were casually swatting away a fly. 'Joel, my lad, love is not always a feeling. Sometimes it's a decision.'

'But . . .' stammered Tom.

Jim smiled, teeth clamped on pipe resolutely. 'Don't worry,' he said from the corner of his mouth, looking around the room at each of them in turn, his eyes sparkling. 'I said *if all else fails*. But I know you won't fail.'

Tom knew it wasn't up for discussion. Jim brewed some tea and brought out a huge rhubarb and custard cake, still warm from the oven, which he served in generous slabs with cream, and the conversation moved on to Rufus Clay and his possible motivation for killing the Queen, and then back to the plan for the following day, until the darkening shadows outside the window told Tom it was time to head home.

As he steered *Maggot* back across the lake, a low half-moon was rising behind Raven Howe, and Tom tried to picture in his mind the events that were about to unfold in the next twenty-four hours. He could imagine vivid streaks of smoke emanating from the peaks; the missiles noiselessly swooping down from three sides; a sudden screaming roar, and then impact.

The sound of the propeller bubbling away behind him was soothing. But he had a nagging sense that he had overlooked something – that there was some piece of information he had allowed to slip away. Like trying to bring up a forgotten name to match to a familiar face, he knew it was there, but he couldn't reach it.

And he knew his plan was hopeless. There were too many unknowns, too many weak links. He needed a safety net that, however drastic, would protect the *Teal*, and all her passengers – including Jim Rothwell – from harm. *If all else fails*, Jim had said, he would be willing to die to protect the Queen. Tom remembered, with horror, how the *Clementine* had been overwhelmed within seconds. There was nothing Jim would be able to do to save the Queen if the attack on the *Teal* came the same way. Which meant only one thing: Tom must not fail. But how? In the end, the drones were no more than eyes. How could they compete with the technology of experts like Rufus Clay and his terrorist organization, whoever they were? How had he been so stupid as to leave the memory card exposed like that? He felt the urge to lash out at something or someone, to throw Snakey's slate with its pathetic skull and crossbones back in his stupid face.

He looked across at Maggie, who was huddled in the bow, her arms wrapped around Archie's neck. The dog pulled his head away from her and yawned. Then, as if it were catching, Maggie yawned too, long and deep, and shut her eyes.

Instantly, Tom knew what he had to do. With a twist of his wrist, he powered up to half throttle and no one spoke over the roar of the engine until they were back on the stone walls of the harbour at Cedar Holme. They arranged to meet at eight the next morning. Then Tom disappeared into the workshop and closed the door firmly behind him.

CHAPTER 20

Tom was leaning over the bow rails of the *Teal*. He was flying, the wind lashing his hair, cold spray in his face, as the boat lurched over the water. But he was tight with fear, not laughing in exhilaration as he remembered he had been before. He grabbed the cold metal of the railings with white knuckles. The boat was too high above the water, travelling impossibly fast, bounding off the waves like a dinghy. He looked for his father behind him, but there on the bridge was Rufus Clay, spinning the wheel like a madman. On the fore-deck, Snakey was presenting the Queen with a huge silvery fish on a platter. The fish had a bomb inside it. He opened his mouth to scream, but his voice was a hoarse whisper that was whipped away by the wind. The fish burst into flames, and instantly the whole boat was on fire. The Queen was engulfed in black smoke but, high above on the bridge, Tom could still see Rufus Clay spinning the wheel, laughing as the boat began to sink. Someone was saying his name: 'Tom. Tom. Wake up!'

Maggie was leaning over him. 'It's OK, Tom. You were having a bad dream.'

'What's the time?' he asked, rubbing his eyes.

'Nearly eight o'clock. What time did you go to sleep?'

'Six, I think.'

'You were yelling something about a fish.'

Tom had worked furiously all night, sawing, drilling, soldering, programming. Then testing and retesting and testing again, until he was too exhausted to do anything but curl up on the old sofa, as the sun was breaking over the eastern fells.

Maggie looked around the workshop with wide eyes. The custard-coloured teddy that had sat on the corner of Tom's bed since he was a toddler was sitting on a workbench, covered in little darts, like a pin cushion. On another bench there was a smoking soldering iron, a couple of hacksaws, a blowtorch and a scattering of syringes. Strewn on the floor were bits of sawn-up metal tube of different lengths, Aunt Emily's hair dryer and the remains of some brown goose feathers. An air compressor hissed softly in a corner.

On the long workbench near the window, three

drones stood in a line: *Skylark* and two multi-rotors. Each had been painted a matt grey and were plugged into charging sockets. Behind each drone was a computer monitor and keyboard. Maggie's nostrils flared and she propped the door open with a fire extinguisher.

'This place stinks.' She pulled a dart out of the bear and it slumped on its side, as if dead. She looked at the dart suspiciously. Its tip was a short section of hollow needle, the kind used for injections, stuck into a rubber bung, with a neat array of goose feathers for a tail.

There were footsteps on the gravel path, and Joel appeared in the doorway. 'Wow,' he said, looking around. 'You've been busy.'

Tom swung his legs over the sofa and ran a hand through his hair.

'After thinking it through last night, I realized the plan had too many holes. The people we are dealing with are not a bunch of schoolboys like Snakey's SBS. They're pros. What if they don't come quietly when we turn up pretending to be the police? What if they don't care? Maybe they're like the suicide bombers you see on the news.'

'Willing to sacrifice everything for their cause,' put in Maggie. 'I wondered about that too.'

'Exactly. Or what if they can disable the drones? Shoot us down or jam the control signal? Or even track us to our base? It's too risky.'

'So you think we need a "nuclear option"?' said Joel,

looking at the bear with interest.

'It's probably best if I show you.'

Tom placed *Skylark* on the floor and sat at its screen. The workshop filled with wind as the drone lifted slowly off the ground. Tom watched the two faces that appeared on the screen as they noticed the cluster of metal tubes, like sawn-off shotguns, that had sprouted overnight from the centre of the machine. The drone stopped in front of the bear. The blinking red light caught in its eyes and gave it a startled expression. Tom pressed a button and there was a pneumatic hiss, like a sharp intake of breath, followed by a pop, and the dart struck the bear where its heart would be.

The weapon was sickeningly quiet. The others watched him solemnly, as he landed the drone and shut it down. Outside, a blackbird was singing cheerfully in the garden. 'It was kind of your idea, Maggie. You asked if it had any weapons.'

'I guess that will do for the nuclear option,' said Joel. 'But what about the other two terrorists?'

Tom gestured to the two other drones, each parked innocently in front of its own monitor, each with its new weapon.

'Listen carefully, because we don't have long and we can't afford to get anything wrong. We agreed that the reason there are three people on three trig points is probably to give them a better chance of getting a hit between them. But can you see what that means?'

'They only need to get one hit to be successful,' said

139

Joel. 'Which means—'

'That we have to take all three down—'

'At exactly the same time.'

'Joel, let him finish,' said Maggie.

'He's right, anyway. We have to coordinate our attack exactly. And that's the tricky bit. We can't fly straight to the trig points. The place will be crawling with security people and if they spot some unidentified UAVs in the airspace over the Queen's route, they'll take action. They can jam the control signals easily, or even shoot us down if they have to. So we'll need to take a detour, fly to a position out of sight of each of the peaks, then we can attack at exactly the same time. I've worked out all the timings.'

Maggie was looking at him with laser eyes, but a flicker of doubt passed across her face.

'There are four rounds on each drone,' Tom continued. 'One shot will administer a dose of a fast-acting anaesthetic, which will put the terrorists out for just long enough for the *Teal* to sail out of range. The other three are in case anyone misses.'

Maggie opened her mouth, and then shut it again.

'Because of battery power,' Tom went on, 'we have no margin of error. Twenty minutes tops for the hexacopters.'

He paused to check they were following him. Maggie looked anxious. But he knew the worst was yet to come.

'I'm sure you'll have thought of it, Tom,' said Joel, 'but if the batteries only last twenty minutes, there won't be enough juice to get the drones back home.'

'You're right,' said Tom. 'I'll come to that. First, there's an even bigger problem. Maggie, Joel. I'm going to have to ask for your help with something.'

'Anything!' said Joel.

'These darts will administer the exact amount to knock out a human adult for fifteen minutes. I checked online, and tested them with water. But water is not going to put these guys to sleep. I need the proper stuff.'

'Propofol would do the job,' said Joel. 'Dad always carries a bottle of it for an emergency anaesthetic. I've seen him knock out full-grown horses with the stuff, so it should be fine for our terrorists!'

Maggie held out her palms in refusal. 'No, Joel. No way. Sorry, Tom, but Dad will lose his job. He could even be put in prison. There are strict rules about these things. Get the dose even a tiny bit wrong and those people are dead.'

'I know. But we won't get the dose wrong.'

Maggie shook her head. 'It's a crazy idea. What if one of the drones falls into the wrong hands, and someone traces the anaesthetic back to us? That would be the end for Dad.'

'Maggie.' Tom looked her straight in the eye. 'The last thing I want is for your dad to end up in jail. Look.' With his stick he scratched the shape of the lake in the rough floor of the workshop, and drew a circle opposite Dowth-waite Bay. 'This point here is the deepest part of one of the deepest lakes in England. It will be a one-way mission.'

141

'I don't understand,' said Maggie. There was a tremble in her voice.

'As Joel said, the multi-rotors won't have enough power to bring them back. But they will have just enough power to fly over the lake. Then we'll nosedive all three drones into the water. They'll be two hundred feet down within seconds. No one will ever see them again. And no one will ever know about using your dad's anaesthetic.'

Maggie stared at the place on the map where the end of Tom's stick was still pointing. She stood up and went to the door.

'I'm sorry, Tom, but it's just too risky. You'll have to think of something else for your nuclear option.'

CHAPTER 21

Tom slammed the workshop doors behind him, and went to the river. He picked up a rock the size of a brick and heaved it as far and as high as he could, letting out a roar like a shot-putter. But the water just made a gulping sound as it swallowed it, as if refusing to acknowledge his frustration.

He was suddenly exhausted. His eyes were blurry and his muscles ached from working, tense and jittery, in his workshop all night. And all he had to show for it was the power to prick someone with a needle, unless he could get hold of some anaesthetic.

He lay down on the grass and watched the circles

ripple towards him, and then all was quiet. Weightless insects rafted across the current. Tom had always found the river calmed him. Its size, its reliability, the mind-boggling power that had engraved its course in the valley. He watched a moss-covered stick circle slowly downstream and drift out of sight.

Just like that stick, he thought, this moment in time, which seemed so immense right now, would soon be gone, swallowed up and forgotten like all the others.

Tom woke to the sound of barking, and felt Archie snuffling around his feet. He pushed himself into a sitting position to see Joel holding out a mug of coffee in one hand and a chocolate muffin in the other.

'Thanks.'

Maggie was sitting on the bank. Tom hoped she'd changed her mind about the anaesthetic, but he glanced over at her, where she was dangling her feet in the water, and her face was hard. She threw a stick for Archie, who jumped in with a clumsy splash, sending some ducks into a panic. He returned and clambered out, spraying water over them, and dropped the stick at Maggie's feet.

'Tom,' said Maggie without warning. 'Tell us about Jim.'

Tom was about to take a swig of coffee, but froze with the mug halfway to his mouth. 'What do you want to know?'

'How did you get to know him?'

'He's kind of retired now, but works as a handyman at my school. Doing odd jobs, fixing things. "Keeping things shipshape" is what he calls it. After I started at the school, somehow a rumour got round about me. It was a total lie, but it went right round the school.'

'What kind of rumour?' said Joel.

'Joel!' said Maggie, glaring at her brother. 'You don't have to tell us, Tom.'

He took a sip of his coffee. He was watching a clump of dried grasses meandering in the current, but he could feel their eyes on him. 'It was about my dad,' he said. 'I don't think I've explained to you, have I? The reason I live here with Aunt Emily is because my mum died when I was little and my dad is an RAF pilot who is officially missing in action.'

'Wow,' said Joel.

'That must be terrible, Tom,' said Maggie, putting a hand on his arm.

'Anyway, when Dad's Tornado had been shot down, people said he had been abandoned by the British government because he was a spy or something. So I used to go to this storeroom that was full of old desks and sit and design things. Jim came in one lunchtime and found me, and we started talking.'

'What happened to his wife?' said Maggie. 'I saw the photos on the wall of his boat.'

'Jim and Lizzie were working in the Congo, helping to run a school. They were like parents to hundreds of children. One day some bandits broke into their house, shot Lizzie in the head and ransacked the place. There was nothing worth stealing, apart from the wedding ring on her finger.'

Archie was watching the stick in Maggie's hand, barking and wagging his tail. 'Go on, Tom,' she said.

'One of the bandits, a fifteen year old, had been to the school,' Tom continued. 'Jim and Lizzie had taken him in from the streets and cared for him like he was their own child. The police rounded some of them up eventually. And here's the thing that you need to know about Jim Rothwell.' He suddenly found he had to clear his throat. 'Jim went to see the boy in prison.'

'Why?' asked Maggie.

'To offer him forgiveness.'

He picked up a handful of pebbles from the ground and scattered them into the water.

They started to head back to the workshop but Maggie disappeared towards River's Edge. She returned ten minutes later and, without meeting his eyes, placed a small brown bottle into Tom's palm.

Back in the workshop Tom checked the clock and the weather, and decided there was enough time to do a practice run of the manoeuvres they would need to do later. Maggie had never flown a UAV, and Joel's one attempt had ended in disaster, so he felt some training would be essential.

He selected some trees further up the Elleray to serve as practice targets. Maggie and Joel each sat behind their screens, with Tom looking over their shoulders, controlling his drone from a tablet.

'There's so much to think about,' said Maggie,

checking her speed and altitude.

Tom scanned the screens, keeping an eye out for anything suspicious on the roads, but there was only the usual stream of holiday traffic mixed in with delivery vans and the occasional tractor. The sky was grey, the landscape below dull and flat.

'The weather's perfect,' he said. 'No shadows.'

'This is one of the weirdest experiences I have ever had,' said Maggie. 'Here we all are, and miles away, in a completely different place, we have the power to put three people to sleep.'

'It's like we're right there,' agreed Joel. 'I could get hooked on this!'

'OK,' said Tom. 'Fire on my command. Three . . .' His voice seemed to be cracking and sweat was trickling down the back of his neck. 'Two . . .' Maggie's knuckles were white on the keyboard. 'One . . .' Joel looked calm but was concentrating hard, like someone sitting an exam.

'And—'

Just then, the door cracked open and Aunt Emily, wearing a blue-and-white dress and red neck scarf, popped her head into the workshop door.

'Here you all are!' she said. 'I'm going across to Watertop Pier to see if I can catch a glimpse of the Queen. Why don't you all get down there instead of sitting in the shed playing computer games?'

They held their drones hovering in position, agonized looks on their faces.

'Actually, Emily,' Maggie explained through gritted teeth, 'we are hoping to see her later. We're just . . . er . . .'

'. . . making our plans for the day,' finished Joel.

'I see.' She adjusted her scarf. 'I know it's silly and I probably won't get anywhere near her, but I can't help feeling I need to dress up a bit. It's going to be a day to remember!'

For a tense few seconds they waited for the workshop door to bang shut.

'Fire!' shouted Tom.

CHAPTER 22

After the practice, Tom got to work with a syringe, carefully dosing each dart with anaesthetic, before handing the bottle back to Maggie, whose parents were out visiting one of Wordsworth's houses and would not return till the evening. Then, with shaking hands, he loaded the twelve metal tubes with the darts.

They talked through the mission. First the journey out, then the attack itself, then the kamikaze-style ending, when they would plunge the machines into a vertical dive into the lake.

At 2.35 p.m. Tom stood up. 'Maggie, Joel: positions.'

He pressed the button to open the skylight, and on his signal the drones lifted up one by one and disappeared into the grey sky.

Anyone stumbling into the workshop at that moment would have seen the tension in the room: backs hunched over screens; faces ferociously concentrating; fingers clenched on controls. Even Archie paced restlessly about, while Tom directed the mission from a wheeled office chair, beads of sweat on his forehead.

Tom never expected to see *Skylark* again, but as the drone disappeared through the roof for the last time, and he glimpsed his own face on the screen, he caught himself inexplicably smiling. A week ago he'd been like a bear in a cave. Now he was surrounded by friends, working together to do something that mattered. And it felt good.

Joel had the longest journey. He was to take *Skylark* west for two and a half miles, then turn south, following a wide loop over Grizedale Forest, before bending east towards Rigg Knott on the western shore.

Meanwhile, Maggie's hexacopter was beginning a long northern climb to avoid the horseshoe of hills behind Watertop, then a sharp turn eastwards, and a descent to the back of Raven Howe. She held the controls with delicate fingers like an artist doing some fine brushwork.

So he could help the others, Tom had chosen Brock-barrow, the closest of the summits.

The whine of the drones faded and Tom scanned the

screens in silence. Maggie was soon clear of the village and was following the line of Perch Beck, milk-white after the recent rain, winding its way down the valley. A few seconds later, the farms and woods had given way to black rock and screes, as she climbed the steep sides of the fell.

'Tom, take a look at this.' Joel was pointing to a vehicle moving along a minor road on the western side of the lake. 'It's the ice cream van.'

'Are you sure?'

The van went out of sight with a twist of the road, but when it reappeared Joel zoomed in through the windscreen, and they caught the unmistakable profile of Mike McCain driving the van, and next to him in the passenger seat was Rufus Clay.

'They're turning into that castle,' said Joel.

'Blythe Castle. There'll be a perfect view from up there. They'll see the *Teal* as she comes out of Dowthwaite Bay. But if those two are in the van . . . who's at the trig points?'

Tom's drone had arrived at the holding point and below was the empty summit of Brockbarrow. 'No one here!'

'Nor at Raven Howe,' said Maggie. 'It's deserted.'

Tom looked at the clock on the wall. It was 2.50 p.m.

'They still have thirteen minutes. But why leave it so late? And what's Rufus Clay doing at Blythe Castle?'

'Tom, shall I change course and keep the van in sight for a while?' asked Joel.

'OK, just for a minute. Head thirty degrees east and keep at that altitude. We mustn't let them spot us.'

As *Skylark* banked around, Blythe Castle came into view again and the top of the lake behind it. The steep-sided Dowthwaite Bay was hidden from view, but there was no hiding the presence of the royal visitor. The northern end of the lake looked as if a giant had waded out and swept a hand across the water in a huge arc. On one side of the arc was a segment of clear water marked by a line of patrol boats and police RIBs, blue lights blinking along the rim: the security cordon. Behind this barrier was a thick band of at least a hundred boats jostling for a view, their churning wakes spreading outwards like a bloom of mould.

'Tom, look at this.' From above Raven Howe, Maggie pointed to where they could see an orange speedboat, stationary behind the white froth of the flotilla. 'It's our red-headed friend, Dr Victoria Juniper, in the *Invincible*.'

'Maybe she's keeping an eye on things from the lake?' suggested Tom.

He turned back to Joel's screen. The ice cream van was parked in the car park in front of the castle overlooking the lake. It had its awning up and an adult and a small child were making their way over to the van.

'What's happening? How can they launch an attack without being there?'

'It's genius, isn't it?' said Joel.

'What?' said Tom.

watch. It was 2.57 p.m. The distance to the flotilla and the security cordon seemed impossible. He looked up. The clouds were thinning and there were patches of blue. *Skylark* was up there somewhere, looking down. Maggie and Joel would be watching. He felt his resolve tighten. He only had one chance.

From a distance the flotilla had looked like a solid wall, but now it was a clutter of boats of all shapes and sizes moving about in different directions, like the organized chaos at the beginning of a sailing race. Cruisers and yachts were pushing their way to the front, while dinghies and hire boats and kayaks bobbed and darted around them. A line of children and instructors in canoes had formed a raft and were edging their way through the mass. All eyes were fixed across the clear space of water to the entrance of the bay, where now, at exactly three o'clock, the elegant shape of the *Teal* emerged.

Tom looked up and saw the first seagull, black against the brightening sky. It was wheeling in a wide circle high above the water. He scanned the air to his left and saw another join it from the eastern shore, gliding in a straight line, and then turn sharply to join the circuit. Then, appearing overhead, came the third, joining from the north. Now all three seagulls were locked in sync, gliding at equal distance from each other, circling down. With robotic precision they came together into a tight circle, wing tips almost touching, and spiralled towards the *Teal*.

When he was close enough to the flotilla to be able to make eye contact with some of the boaters, Tom pushed the tiller and *Maggot* curved away to port. He had to get himself noticed as a threat. Then, if he could draw some police boats away from the security cordon, he hoped that would create an opening for him to get to the *Teal*.

He swerved between boats at full speed, soaking a couple in a rowing boat with spray. People began to shout at him, but he kept the throttle on full. He could see the line of police launches, wardens and black RIBs guarding the rim of the cordon at the front. At last one of them noticed him and he heard the wail of a siren. A police launch, blue lights flashing, was pushing through the boats from the cordon towards him, opening a strip of clear water. He cut the throttle, turned round and waited. As the police launch came level he twisted the throttle, gunned *Maggot* through the corridor of clear water and broke through the security cordon. He now had a clear view of the *Teal*, steaming out into the lake, and above were the three black shapes of the seagull drones, corkscrewing down on their prey.

It was 3.02 p.m. and all he had to do was hold his course at this speed and head straight for the *Teal*, forcing her to change her own course, and causing the drones to miss their target. Ignoring shouts and sirens behind him, Tom kept his eyes on the *Teal* and pushed towards her. There was the sound of a ship's horn, five quick blasts for danger. The *Teal* shuddered and belched black smoke from the funnels as the engines were rammed astern. He broke into a smile as he realized she was changing course.

But suddenly there was another boat cutting across his bow, making him change direction. He tried to swerve around it but it was faster and he had to slow down. It had no police markings or lights, though it was forcing him to stop, and was now heading towards him, matching his turns, like a game of chicken. In the confusion of boats and noise and water Tom could hardly take it in, but as they came closer together he could see that it was *Stingray*. Snakey was at the wheel, jaw locked in defiance, and for a moment their eyes met. Tom cut the engine and slammed the tiller away, sending spray ripping into Snakey's face as *Maggot* came to a shuddering stop pressed up against *Stingray*'s sides.

Everyone was looking at him. Another boat was coming alongside. Someone was climbing into *Maggot* and putting a hand on his shoulder.

Tom was still watching the *Teal*. He could see Jim Rothwell now, wearing a suit, hands on the railings looking at him. The Queen was nowhere to be seen on deck, but he saw a scrum of people inside the cabin. He searched the air above, and just off the *Teal*'s port bow three white-and-grey shapes, wings folded into a dive, plunged into the water.

Jim smiled, and, without moving his hands from the railings, raised his thumbs in the air. Mission accomplished.

An armed policeman, his gloved hand gripping Tom's

shoulder, lifted the visor of his combat helmet. 'What's your name, boy?'

Tom's throat was dry. Guns were pointing at him from a RIB, police in full-body armour, radios squawking. He swallowed hard.

'Just tell me your name, please.'

'Thomas Hopkins.'

'Thomas Hopkins, I'm arresting you on suspicion of terrorism offences. Please put your hands on your head and lie on the floor of the boat.'

CHAPTER 23

Dinner was nearly over by the time Maggie realized that her parents did not believe them. Her mum had cheerfully made Maggie's favourite meal, but she could barely taste the prawn laksa in front of her.

She had been in turmoil since Tom's arrest. Joel had been infuriatingly silent. She knew his mind was racing too but she could get nothing out of him. They had sat miserably in the workshop to analyse the footage Joel had taken from *Skylark*, starting from when they heard *Maggot*'s roaring engine disappear round the bend in the river.

And there they were: three streaks of white over the glittering water. Pure as doves, soaring on the afternoon thermals, wings stretched out, heads still, eyes on the prey below.

'It's brilliant,' said Maggie, shaking her head. 'They just blend in like real seagulls. No one would even know what had hit them.'

'No,' said Joel.

'Just as Tom said.'

'Yes,' he said.

'Unbelievable.'

'Yes,' he said again. 'It is.'

'Look, there he is,' she said, as *Maggot* emerged into view and they watched it all again: the reckless rip through the flotilla, the corridor opening up, the police launch surging behind, the black speedboat barring the way.

'Watch.' Joel manually slowed the replay of the film. They focused on each jerky moment, frame by frame, with a terrible fascination: they saw the *Teal* go into reverse, foam billowing behind like suds from a demented washing machine; the figures on deck bundle towards the cabin, dark suits surrounding a lilac hat; then the armed RIBs tilting in towards a single small boat, like iron filings to a magnet, then the arrest, a circle of guns, a tightening ring of spectators. And as the *Teal* began to reverse, three bird-like weapons, in perfect formation, folded their wings, and sliced into the water no more than fifteen feet away from the bow, with barely a splash.

'This is so annoying!' said Maggie. 'It looks like a scene from a wildlife documentary, not a terrorist attack. No one will believe this is anything.'

'No,' Joel had said again. 'No, they won't.'

Now, around the scrubbed pine table in River's Edge, Maggie was all too aware of how unbelievable it sounded. Her parents listened to their story without saying a word. Maggie's dad leant across the table and helped himself – a little too cheerfully, Maggie thought – to another ladle of soup. 'Now Tom's being questioned by the authorities, I'm sure they'll be able to get to the bottom of it all.'

Maggie placed her chopsticks on the table with infinite care. Joel did his rotating-turret look, moving his gaze from his dad to his sister.

'What do you mean, "get to the bottom of it all"?' she said.

Her mum interjected. 'He just means, Maggie, they'll try and help him.'

'Help him?'

'Yes,' said her mum. 'That's what the boy needs. Help.'

'Help for what? Help investigating a terrorist attack that has been wrongly pinned on him, you mean?'

Maggie's dad's face darkened. 'Now, Maggie, there's no need to be sarcastic. Anyone can see that Tom has had a difficult few years. He's been left parentless, moved home, moved schools, then suffered some sort of injury, and who knows what else? These things traumatize people and when people are traumatized their grasp on reality is sometimes damaged. It could happen to anyone.'

'Are you saying we've imagined all this as well?' asked Maggie.

'I'm not making any judgment about anyone. But let's think about what it looks like from the outside. What exactly have you seen or heard yourselves that convinced you the Queen was going to be attacked by terrorists on a boat trip? Is it not possible that you all got carried away with Tom's theory?'

'Theory? Dad, we've seen things, heard things! We haven't just made this all up. And –' Maggie inhaled deeply and looked squarely at her dad – 'you'll just have to take our word for it.'

Her mum stood up and began to clear the table. 'Even if you're right, Maggie, we're not going to help him by falling out about it.'

The only sound for some time was the clink of bowls and cutlery.

'At least the terrorists can't get to him while he's locked up,' Joel said at last.

Their mum let out a sigh. 'Stop being melodramatic, Joel. He's just being assessed. He's not in prison.'

'And who *are* these terrorists?' asked their dad, palms open. 'All that actually took place, as far as anyone can see, is that a troubled teenage boy went berserk and tried to ram his boat into the steamer with the Queen on board. That's what it looks like, and that's how the police

162

will have to treat it. They have nothing else to go on.'

'We know that's how it looks, Dad,' said Maggie. 'But things aren't always the way they look. Tom was trying to save the boat, not ram it.'

Her dad stood up and picked up an iPad from the kitchen side.

'Here it is: *Youth Foils Royal Attack.*'

'Oh!' said Maggie, brightening.

'Listen,' he said, shaking his head. '*A quick-thinking youth is being praised by police after his courageous intervention prevented an alleged attempt to attack a vessel with Her Majesty the Queen on board. The incident occurred in the Lake District at the beginning of a Royal Tour, earlier today. After opening the new Freshwater Biology Study Centre at Dowthwaite Bay, the Queen was travelling on board the historic boat,* MV Teal, *accompanied by a variety of special guests, including local celebrity chef, Brian Wilkins. The incident occurred three minutes into the cruise. Thirteen-year-old Ryan Snaith spotted a fast-moving motorboat breaching the security cordon and intercepted it—*'

'No way!' Maggie banged her hand on the table. 'This is unbelievable.'

Her dad glanced at her over the tablet, and carried on. '*Thirteen-year-old Ryan Snaith spotted a fast-moving motorboat breaching the security cordon and intercepted it, preventing an alleged attempt to ram the royal vessel. The driver of the motorboat, another local youth, who can't be named for legal reasons, was apprehended by waterborne royal protection officers.*

'Deputy Chief Constable Mark Robertson told the BBC that the attack was believed to be a one-off incident. "The boy claimed he was preventing some sort of terrorist plot. But he was unable to provide any evidence for this," Robertson explained. "The youth is being detained under anti-terror laws, until we have ruled out possible extremist connections."'

He closed the tablet and looked at Maggie. 'We want to believe you, Maggie. But do you have any hard evidence?'

Maggie's mum stopped clearing the table. In the silence Maggie's mind ran over everything that had happened in the past week: from Mike McCain selling ice creams in the car park at Dowthwaite Bay, to her close escape on Benson Isle, to the attack itself. But what would count as proof? It boiled down to two things. There was the chip with photographs clearly showing criminal activity – which Snakey had stolen from the kitchen windowsill. And there was the video that Joel had taken from *Skylark* showing three seagulls diving into the water – which is what seagulls did.

Her mum walked the pile of bowls over to the sideboard. She returned to the table and looked at Maggie, eyebrows arched, echoing her husband's question.

'No, we don't,' said Maggie. 'Not yet.'

CHAPTER 24

After dinner Maggie rowed out in *Bobalong* to the spot where the seagull-drones had nosedived. She stretched out with each stroke, a cleansing breeze in her hair. The rhythm of the effort began to unclutter her mind, though she was still fuming about the injustice of it all. She looked at the sky pensively, but there was just the dome of pale blue and a band of high clouds bottom-lit by the evening sun. She was about to turn for home when she saw Jim Rothwell coming towards her in *Swallow*, the blades of his oars scooping up shavings of light. He looked over his shoulder and nodded, unsurprised, pipe in his mouth. He was still three or four strokes away when she caught the aromatic trail of smoke: a mix of fresh straw, cloves, burnt toast. The grown-up scent reached out to her on the evening breeze like an invisible arm of kindness.

'Lovely evening for a row,' he said, coming alongside. 'Sometimes you just need to clear your head, don't you?'

'Yeah,' she said, grabbing hold of *Swallow*'s gunwale. 'It's so unfair, Jim. If it weren't for Tom, the Queen would be dead and the *Teal* would be at the bottom of the lake. But who gets praised from the rooftops?'

'I know. I've seen the news.' He let the smoke curl around him. Behind, the hills were glowing in the evening sun.

'What are we going to do?'

'Do?'

'About the terrorists, Snakey, Tom being treated like a criminal!'

'We could start by being thankful, I suppose.'

'Thankful?'

'Don't forget, Maggie, you achieved what you set out to do. As you said yourself, the Queen is alive and well, and the *Teal* is still sailing these tranquil waters as if nothing happened. Mission accomplished. I presume you didn't do it to be "praised from the rooftops"?'

'No, but—'

'You know, Maggie, saving other people usually comes at a price. Tom may have made himself look a bit daft for now. But, as I always say, "the truth will out in the end". You'll see.'

'And I guess he's in a safe place.'

'I'm told that he is being well cared for, yes. But I intend to see for myself. I have an appointment with the Deputy Chief Constable first thing in the morning and I'm going to see if I can vouch for Tom's character and get him back home. I need to be careful, though. If – and I think it's a big if – the authorities are mixed up in this, then there's always a danger that saying too much will alert the terrorists that we're on to them. As for that Snaith lad, don't worry about him. His day will come.'

Maggie looked across the lake to the summit of Raven Howe. 'Why does he hate Tom so much anyway, Jim?'

'Hurt people, hurt people,' he said simply, raising an eyebrow to check she understood.

Maggie shook her head, bewildered.

He pointed the tip of his pipe towards her and began to chuckle. 'You see, Maggie, Tom Hopkins and Ryan Snaith have more in common than you might think. When I first met Tom, he was a strange, damaged creature. I took it as coldness at first but then I realized that he was like . . . like an egg. A hollow shell that could crack at any moment. After some time, he told me why. And there was a time when Ryan Snaith was like that too. On the brink, trying to work out who he was. Sadly, he chose the wrong path. But Tom could easily have lost his way too.'

'But he hasn't, has he?'

'No, Maggie, and in part, that's thanks to this whole

business, and to you and your brother turning up at just the right time. In a strange kind of way this little escapade is exactly the jolt he needed to stop brooding on his own problems and think about someone else. Which he did, I might add, spectacularly!'

He slotted the pipe back in his mouth with a clash of teeth, and looked at her.

It was true that Tom had risked himself to save others. They had not had time to discuss it. But, Snakey or no Snakey, he would still have looked like a lunatic breaking through the cordon and charging towards the *Teal*. He'd counted the cost.

A lawnmower-like hum made them look up. A microlight, gossamer wings backlit in the last rays, was drifting overhead.

'I saw those birds hit the water a few yards off the port bow and it all made perfect sense. No one else had worked it out – all these police and MI5 and who knows what else, with millions of pounds in resources and access to global intelligence, and they completely missed what a thirteen-year-old boy saw from his garden shed. So cheer up.'

Maggie pushed the fringe out of her eyes and looked straight at Jim. 'The problem is no one believes us and we have no proof.'

He looked at the bowl of his pipe, where the little bed of embers was fading, and reached into a pocket for a box of matches. 'What do you have in mind?'

'A bit of digging, before the trail goes cold.'

'Where will you start?'

Maggie shrugged, and pulled one of the oars further into the boat before it slipped out of its rowlock. 'What do you know about Hollowdale?'

'It's very remote. The Thirlmere Aqueduct passes right under the fellside there. But why do you ask? If that's where you think these people are, I'd advise you to stay well away!'

'What's the Thirlmere Aqueduct?'

He gestured to the north with a nod. 'There's an enormous man-made reservoir up the valley there. Thirlmere. The Victorians built it to provide Manchester with water almost one hundred miles away, which it still does. The water flows downhill through the longest man-made underground aqueduct in the world. Did you know that? Amazing, those Victorians.'

'I had no idea. And we live in Manchester too.'

'Yes. "You never miss the water till the well runs dry," as the saying goes.' Jim pulled a match out of the box, struck it and relit his pipe, cupping his hands against the dying breeze. 'But listen to me, Maggie. Whatever else you do to help Tom, don't go walking into the lion's den!'

After getting ready for bed, Maggie sat on the balcony of River's Edge, the mellow evening air clinging to her skin. She sat with her book unopened on her lap and listened to the river sighing softly below, as if getting ready for sleep.

She thought about what Jim had said about not going to Hollowdale. He was right, of course. And yet, if no one ever went near the lion's den, as he called it, those people would get away with everything.

A female goosander with some newly hatched chicks was labouring upstream, orange tufts glistening with jewels of water from a recent dive. Maggie counted the chicks. There were eight, or possibly nine or even ten. It was impossible to be sure because they were all following the mother so closely, in a tightly packed clump, legs beating twice as fast as hers to keep up.

As she watched the birds disappear around the bend, three kayakers came into view, paddling downstream towards her. As they came close, Maggie shrank back into the shadows of the overhanging roof and held her breath. Each of them wore a black diving suit and had a diving mask and snorkel draped around their neck. The slender grey kayaks were studded with pieces of equipment fixed with straps. When they came level with the boathouse, she recognized Victoria Juniper. One of the others turned his head slightly and she spotted the man with the ponytail, Mike McCain. The third one, a younger man with a deep tan and tattoos all over his arms, she'd never seen before. None of them spoke, but she could hear the rhythmic splashing of the paddles long after they had disappeared out of sight behind the reeds on the next bend. Maggie breathed out, and felt goosebumps creep up her arms. She looked out at the eddies and bubbles that were closing up the path left by the kayakers, like a scar healing over, and decided to disregard Jim's advice. If she couldn't find the guts to go to Hollowdale, she wondered if her world would ever feel safe again.

CHAPTER 25

The following morning, Maggie and Joel were sitting on the balcony at River's Edge with mugs of tea on a cast iron table in front of them. Maggie described the three terrorists she had seen kayaking down the river the previous evening in full diving gear.

'They were obviously doing something underwater, further up the river, but what?'

'I have no idea, Joel, but it freaked me out. I had nightmares about them climbing into the house and dragging me off in their canoes to some hideout in the middle of the lake.'

'You think too much, Maggie,' said Joel. 'I slept like a baby.'

'Well, it's time to think now,' said Maggie, shoving him in the shoulder so he nearly fell off his chair. 'Go and get the map, lazybones. It's time we checked out that farm at Hollowdale. It's the one lead we have to go on.'

Joel fetched an Ordnance Survey map. Archie, who had been resting his head on his paws, watching the ducks in the river, sprang up, sensing action.

'I love the OS 1:25,000 scale,' said Joel, spreading out the map.

'You're such a nerd,' said Maggie.

'I know.'

'But you're right. You can see every detail. Look. There are the islands. You can even see the little islet off the tip of Ransome Holme. Urgh! I so want to punch that Snakey boy. Now, let's find this Hollowdale place.'

They hunched over the map. From Cedar Holme the pale blue ribbon of the Elleray tapered away to the west, while to the north the village of Watertop sat squashed into the centre of a small bowl-shaped valley, with the lake itself to the south. Between the village and the top of the map, a swathe of brown showed the high fells and valleys, arcing round from east to west like the ribs of a fan, each valley with its own ribbon of water heading downwards, as if determined to reach the body of blue to the south. Scattered here and there, patches of green indicated woodland refuge from the relentless march of the contour lines.

Maggie placed her finger on the map and moved it northwards across several of these valleys until it came to a stop in a deep U-shaped trough, framed by jagged ridges.

'There it is,' she said, tapping her finger on the map. 'Hollowdale.'

'It must be that farm there on the hillside,' said Joel. 'There's nowhere else it could be.'

'Tom said it would make a great terrorist HQ,' said Maggie. 'It's not even on a proper road. That dotted line must be a farm track of some sort. The nearest road is that wiggly one there.'

'I'm guessing Mr Clay didn't choose this place for the shopping and nightlife,' said Joel.

'It's the perfect hideout for someone up to no good,' said Maggie. 'No passers-by. And the farm probably has views right down the valley, so they would be able to see anyone coming up that track before they arrive.'

'Which means we need to come at it a different way, so we're not seen,' said Joel. 'But that will add miles to the route. We'll have to take the main road through the village, walk up through those woods, around that tarn and then up that ridge.' He drummed his fingertips on the map. 'At the top we should get a view of the farm, and then we can check it out properly. After all, we don't know for certain that this is their base yet.'

Maggie ran her finger along the route. 'It's quite a long way. And it's going to be baking today, by the looks of it.'

'In which case,' said Joel, 'I think a second breakfast might be in order!'

'I've got a better idea,' said Maggie. 'I'm sure I saw an old tent in the boathouse downstairs.'

An hour later they were packed and ready to go. Joel thought the tarn below the ridge would make a perfect base camp, where they would be well hidden. Maggie suggested getting in touch with Tom to let him know the plan, just in case he was let out before they returned and wondered where they had gone. They tried his mobile but it went straight to voicemail. This, Joel pointed out, was not surprising, given the circumstances. They left a message about what they were planning to do, including the grid references for the tarn where they planned to camp, and Maggie left a note with the same information on it in his workshop.

'Still,' she said, 'it would have been good to hear his voice before we go.'

They found Aunt Emily sitting in the kitchen, a folded newspaper on her lap and a cup of tea on the table. She looked haggard, Maggie thought.

'Do you mind if we speak to you about Tom, Emily?' said Maggie softly. She touched the teacup. It was cold, and a skin of milk had formed on the top. 'Would you like me to make you a fresh cup of tea?' she added.

'Tea? Oh, no, thank you, dear.'

'We tried giving Tom a call. To check he's OK,' said Joel. 'But it went straight to voicemail. Have you heard from him at all?'

'I saw him briefly at the police station but I haven't

spoken to him since then,' said Aunt Emily. She pulled a tissue out of her sleeve and wiped her nose. 'The social worker, who took Thomas with her, said not to get in contact yet.'

'Why not?'

'She said, "don't call for a week". I asked why and she said something about unsettling him.'

Maggie opened her mouth, but Joel cut in before she could speak: 'I suppose they wouldn't want outside contact with inmates at, er . . . what's the place called again?'

'Lindsay House,' she said, creasing the newspaper along its fold. 'It's called Lindsay House Secure Children's Home.'

Maggie and Joel shot each other a look.

'Do you think he'll be coping OK?' asked Maggie after a few moments.

Aunt Emily gathered herself together and looked at Maggie and Joel, as if noticing them for the first time. 'He'll be coping better than I am!' She smiled weakly at them. Maggie noticed the moisture in her eyes. 'So long as he's not cooped up in some small space.'

'How do you mean?' asked Maggie.

'Hasn't he told you about his claustrophobia? Thomas *hates* being in small spaces or underground. It goes back to when he was very small. He got trapped in a coal shed. It was just a silly mistake. Somehow he crawled in and no one noticed he was missing for a while. By the time they did Thomas was hysterical. And since then he's always had this thing about being in enclosed spaces. Or being underground. It's the only thing he's properly scared of.'

'Maybe that's why he loves flying so much,' Joel mused.

'Flying? Yes, I suppose he would, if he had a chance. His father, you know . . .' She broke off, and wiped her eyes with the tissue. 'Anyway, it was underground that he had his accident. There's a geography trip everyone does at his school. Thomas had been dreading it for months. They take you into an old slate mine.'

'What happened?'

'He said he had a panic attack in the tunnel and ended up falling down a ledge or something. The problem is . . .'

'Yes?'

'Well, I wonder if there was more to it. But Thomas never wants to talk about it.'

They went into the garden where Joel googled the number and phoned the institution that was listed. 'Hello,' he said in his deepest voice. 'I'd like to speak to Tom Hopkins, please . . . Thomas Hopkins. Yes, I'll wait.'

Joel looked at Maggie and raised his eyebrows. After half a minute the person on the other end returned.

'What? Tom Hopkins from Watertop. He was admitted on Wednesday. Are you sure? OK. Thanks.' Joel ended the call and stared at the phone. 'She says they have no one registered there by that name.'

'Weird,' said Maggie.

They were heading out of the gate when Aunt Emily

appeared with a laundry basket. 'I'd better get this washing in. There's some heavy weather coming tonight. It's all Thomas's things, ready for when he gets home. They didn't ask him to take any clean clothes. I don't know why.'

Maggie stopped and turned to her suddenly. 'Emily?' she said. 'You know the social worker you handed Tom over to?'

'At the police station? Well, I didn't exactly—'

'But you met her?'

'Yes.'

'What did she look like?'

'Well, dear, now I think about it, I didn't notice very much. I was in a bit of a state, to tell you the truth. It's all such a terrible mistake, you see. Thomas would never deliberately do something so rash. And I was so pleased that he'd found some friends, and he was getting out a bit more. And now this.' She fiddled with the cord attached to her glasses, shaking her head.

'But did you notice anything about the woman?'

'She just seemed perfectly normal, I think. Young. Clever type. Oh, and lovely curly red hair.'

CHAPTER 26

Tom watched a spider crawl across the wall in front of him. It inched its way over the flaking green paint and dropped down to the floor, where it disappeared into a crack in the concrete. In the building above, a pipe hummed and gurgled. There were muffled voices somewhere far away and a metal door slammed shut. He had slept, but he had no idea for how long. He had no way of keeping track of time in the windowless room. They had taken his watch and he had not had his phone since he'd left it in his rucksack in *Maggot* after their encounter with the terrorists on Benson Isle, in the rush to get home with a waterlogged *Skylark*.

That was one of the many sudden flashes of memory and regret that had plagued his mind since the moment he realized it was the terrorists who had collected him from the police station, not a social worker, as everyone had been led to believe. If only he had kept the memory card in sight instead of putting it on the kitchen windowsill, he might not be in this mess now. He could have gone to the police with solid evidence of what these people were up to, and maybe *they* would be behind bars right now, rather than him.

Instead he had been taken to a remote farm and led down to a basement, where he was told he had to tell them what he knew, how he knew it and who else he had told, or they would take him, trussed up like a chicken in the bottom of a boat, and throw his weighted body into the middle of the lake. When he managed to force himself to think clearly, Tom turned this threat over in his mind. What bothered him was the fact that they had not blindfolded him for the journey.

At the police station he had said goodbye to Aunt Emily. She had not said an angry word to him. She'd just looked baffled, and he'd longed to explain everything to her. But they hadn't given him the chance. PC Linda Clark, who kept calling him 'young man' and 'my fine friend', but spoke to him as if he had the mental age of a three year old, had then shown him into the back seat of a Toyota pickup and told him to wait while she and Aunt Emily had 'a little chat' with the social worker, who was waiting for them in another room.

There was a man in the driver's seat in front of him and Tom could see his eyes in the rear-view mirror, but when Tom asked where they were going he didn't speak or turn around. A few minutes later Victoria Juniper got into the passenger seat. The driver, who Tom then realized was Mike McCain, met Tom's stunned reaction with a wink in the mirror, and the car sped off. The click of the central locking was like a gun being cocked.

They drove through the village and up the twisting pass, with buses and cars grinding down in low gear – strangers flashing past feet away, but so far from helping Tom they might as well have been on another planet.

They turned down a farm track, and as the bare valley opened out in front of them he knew where he was. Many times he had flown through Hollowdale, and barely noticed the lonely farm, hunched in the shadows of crevices and crags. So this was their HQ.

As they approached the farm, Tom could see a twelve-foot fence, topped with razor wire. Next to the entrance, in ridiculously cheery comic sans font, a sign announced:

Luscious Lakeland – Real Ice Cream,
Fresh from the Farm.

The gates were opened by a guard with a sub-machine gun, whom he didn't recognize. He began to wonder how many of these people there were. Inside the compound an open-fronted brick barn sheltered an assortment of vehicles: the ice cream van, the two black Land Rovers he had seen at the quarry, a quad bike and a yellow mini dumper truck. As the car came to a halt, a dog's bark boomed around the yard.

Mike McCain, who turned out to be much stronger than he looked, pulled him out of the Toyota before he could grab his stick. He pushed him into a concrete building, dragged him along some corridors and virtually threw him down the steps into the basement, where Tom landed painfully on the floor. Before he could pick himself up, the man came over to him, pulled him up and thrust him into a chair.

'All we want to know is how you knew. That's all. If you tell us that – happy days.' Mike leant closer and Tom got a whiff of breath that made him think of a butcher's shop. 'I'll be back to take you to see the boss, when he's ready. I'm sure you'll open up to him.' Then he was gone, slamming the heavy door, with its prison bars, and locking the deadlock with as much violence as he could throw at it.

A few minutes later, to Tom's relief, the man had returned, said, 'Fetch, doggy,' and tossed his walking stick into a corner of the room. When he left, Tom crawled to the corner and sat on the floor, cradling it in his arms like a baby. But his relief at having his stick was short-lived. The thought that kept niggling him was that he had seen everything. If they ever intended to release him, why not blindfold him or throw him in the back of a van? Tom could only think of one answer to that question, and he realized with a sickening clarity that spilling the beans was not going to get him a ticket out. And – since everyone would assume he was safe in some institute for troubled teenagers, having long chats over hot chocolate with smiling therapists – no one was coming to rescue him.

CHAPTER 27

The route to Hollowdale took Maggie and Joel through Watertop, where they decided to stock up on supplies. In the village they joined the throng of pedestrians trudging along the narrow pavement, scrutinizing café menus, hovering by the windows of outdoor shops with their never-ending sales. No one was in a hurry. They got stuck behind a couple sluggishly pushing a balloon-festooned pram up the hill towards the crossing.

'This is ridiculous,' stated Joel loudly.

'Thanks,' said Maggie as the couple made space for them to pass. 'Honestly, Joel!'

'Well, not everyone has a friend who has been kidnapped by terrorists,' he said hoarsely into Maggie's ear.

As they were passing a tiny house built on a bridge, Archie began to growl, deep in his throat, and slunk down on his haunches. He was looking into a crowd of faces, a blur of tourists milling around with their heads in maps and leaflets.

'What's up, boy?' said Maggie. 'What have you seen?'

Then suddenly they were there, right in her face, so close she could smell the unctuous body spray. There was a new smugness in Snakey's eyes.

'Hello.' He planted his feet on the pavement in front of them, causing a hiker with a small child on his back to swerve into the road. 'Nice day for a camping trip. But hold on, there's someone missing. Oh, no, it's Tom Hop-Hop-Hop-Hop-Hopkins! You haven't left him behind, have you? Doh!' He banged his hand on his forehead. 'Sorry, I forgot, he can't come, can he? Because he's in the funny farm.'

The other two boys laughed. Podge was carrying a motorbike helmet in one hand and in the other an iced latte the size of a small bucket from one of the coffee shops that lined the main street. He looked at Maggie blankly, and licked his white moustache.

Maggie took a deep breath, trying to keep the tremor out of her voice. 'Actually, we were hoping to bump into you guys. You have something that belongs to us and we want it back.'

'Yeah?' Snakey put a finger to his lips. 'And what might that be?'

'Do I need to spell it out? Something small and electronic that you took when you came sneaking around last week?'

'Oh, that? Like I said before, if you want it, come and get it.'

Maggie was thinking hard. If she kept on about the memory card, she would give away how important it was to them. Better to leave it for now and think of a plan to get it back later.

'Come on, Snakey,' said Sam. 'I could slaughter a burger.'

Snakey took a step closer and looked steadily at Maggie. 'We'll be seeing you again soon, losers. And this time, there will be nowhere to hide.'

Maggie felt like something inside her was about to snap. She saw the boy blink as she took a sudden step towards him, but then she felt Joel's hand on her shoulder pulling her back. She bit her lip and walked away so quickly that Joel had to run to catch her up. Fifty yards later she looked back to see Snakey pointing pistol fingers at her before sauntering down the hill.

It was a relief to leave the village behind. They tramped along the pavement for half a mile, and discussed whether they should take Snakey's threat seriously.

'How could they possibly know where we're going? It must have been a stupid threat,' said Maggie.

'Yes,' said Joel uncertainly. 'Although somehow that

186

doesn't seem Snakey's style.'

They turned off the road to follow a path that began to climb north-east, and away from the village. Joel set the pace, map in hand. Archie bounded ahead at first, but as the way became steeper he tired and trotted along at their side. After a while the path joined a stream of smooth pools, but as they climbed higher the water bubbled over hidden rocks into foaming white cauldrons. Before a bend they looked back to see the village, now far below, and the lake a slice of silver, disappearing into a haze. They could see a family of hikers beginning the long trek that they had just covered. Apart from that they were on their own.

'I don't think those clowns will come near us now,' said Maggie decisively. 'They haven't got the guts for a march like this without a McDonald's at the top of every hill. Come on. Forget them. We've got more important things to do.'

For a while the murmur of the stream and their footsteps on the path were the only sounds to accompany their own quickening breaths. A jackdaw coasted past them, its *kyow kyow* bouncing off the rocks.

'*Corvus monedula*,' Joel muttered automatically.

Maggie suddenly stopped dead. 'What if Hollowdale isn't even the right place?'

'And they've taken Tom somewhere else!'

'Come on!' she said, striding forward again. 'Jim says "the truth will out". Let's make sure he's right.'

The path soon entered an old oak wood. After the trek from the village, the change in air was like a cool flannel and their eyes took time to adjust to the shade.

'We can take a shortcut here,' said Joel, looking at the map. 'If we head off the path straight up through this wood, we'll come to a higher path eventually. It'll be hard going for a bit but it'll save us time.'

They had a drink and some Kendal Mint Cake and began to climb directly into the steep wooded hillside. For some time they scrambled over roots and rocks and ducked their heads under lichen-bearded branches. As the gradient became more severe, the oaks gave way to beech and hazel, and beneath them wizened mountain ashes clung to outcrops of limestone. Eventually they joined a distinct bark-chip path curving in from the right, which took them in zigzags through the trees.

Soon the ancient deciduous trees surrendered to larches and Scots pines stretching up to a dense canopy, which shut out light and sound and trapped the resin-scented air below. Even their footsteps were silenced by the drifts of dry needles that covered the floor.

Joel was ahead, compass in hand. 'We should come to the tarn in a few minutes.'

His voice seemed muffled, as if the air were thicker under the trees.

'This silence is weird,' said Maggie. 'It feels like the trees are watching us. As if the whole wood is holding its breath, waiting for something.'

'Come on. We're nearly there.' Joel marched ahead

with Archie at his heels.

Then there was a glow of light ahead and they spilt out into the open so abruptly that they had to shade their eyes. In front of them was a lonely-looking tarn fringed with reeds. On the far side of the tarn, rows of pines rose up steeply towards a ridge of jagged rock. The water was rippled and gave no reflection. The place was eerie and enclosed, and Maggie felt trapped.

'We need to head for that ridge,' said Joel, looking at the map again. 'If there's one thing I've learnt from Tom, it's the importance of getting a bird's-eye view.'

'Emily said it was going to rain,' said Maggie. 'Maybe we should get the tent up first, and then go and work out how we're going to rescue Tom.' She looked across the tarn, where the tops of the pines were shivering in the breeze. Behind the ridge the sky was thick. 'If we've even got the right place.'

CHAPTER 28

Tom put his head in his hands and tried to get a grip on himself, but all he could think about was the double horror of being imprisoned and underground at the same time. He could not imagine a worse situation to be in.

He forced himself to breathe steadily. His prison was a small basement room, every inch of the walls painted an unpleasant kind of green. A single bare bulb threw a circle of dirty yellow light over the table and two chairs.

He began to wonder where the spider had disappeared to. He got down on his hands and knees and put an eye to the crack in the concrete. There was nothing but black, though he could feel the breath of an updraught on the surface of his eyeball.

And there was a scent too. A faint, familiar taste of the outside world, which he couldn't quite place. He pressed his nose to the crack. The smell seemed to suggest an empty cavity below him, of rock and earth and hollow spaces. The flash of memories sent a long, cold shiver through the back of his skull and down his spine until his feet tingled.

Now he put his ear to the crack and the sound he heard far below explained the scent. It was the sound of moving water. Not rushing and tumbling like a mountain stream, or gushing and whining like a pipe. But it was the sound of a vast and endless flow of water, snaking invisibly through the darkness, somewhere deep beneath his feet.

There were footsteps approaching. He went to the door and peered through the bars, straining to hear. But it was just someone walking past the top of the stairwell. Then he caught sight of something glinting against the wall at the top of the stairs. It had to be the key to his cell! If only he could reach it, but there was no way, even with his stick—

Tom felt an electric shock shoot up his spine. Why hadn't he thought of it before? He unscrewed the top of his walking stick with shaking fingers and lifted *Gnat* out of its tube. He looked at the machine, lying in his palm like a sleeping bird, and could have cried at the beautiful sight. The miniature drone looked unharmed and its lolly-stick sized rotor arms sprang into position with a click. He opened the control panel and pushed the throttle. This, he told himself, as he felt the cool breeze of the blades on his cheeks, was going to be a very long shot.

There were more footsteps in the corridor above. Mike McCain had said he'd be back to collect him. Once he was outside that door, *Gnat* was his only chance. He quickly slipped the drone into his pocket and screwed the top back on to his stick as Mike appeared, silhouetted at the top of the staircase. He grabbed the key from the nail, stomped down to the door, unlocked it, and yanked Tom back up the steps. At the top he turned right and dragged Tom along a dim passage with windows looking out to the yard. In the fading daylight he could see vehicles, shiny in the rain, and recognized the Bentley he had seen at the quarry. A low-level humming, little more than a vibration in the soles of his feet, was coming from somewhere in the building. The smell of the place reminded him of school science labs: burnt metal and gas and sulphuric acid, with a background note of floor cleaner. Everywhere was spotlessly clean, like a hospital. No evidence of ice cream making, Tom thought. Mike clamped an arm behind his back and steered him around a corner and down a long corridor, starkly lit by bare bulbs, with a single, unmarked door at the end.

As they approached the door, Mike's boots clopping hard on the polished floor, images of what lay behind that door crowded into Tom's mind: a dark, windowless chamber, full of instruments of torture, some grinning psycho smoking a giant cigar and stroking a cat behind a desk, face bottom-lit blue by flickering screens.

Instead, Mike opened the door without knocking, and pushed Tom into a bright, business-like office. He pointed to a comfortable-looking chair, and turned back to the door. 'Wait there. And don't try anything stupid.' The door shut with a soft click, and to Tom's surprise, he was alone.

The chair, with its cool, leathery smell, seemed to swallow him up. He gripped on to his stick, and glanced warily around the room. In front of him was a large desk, bare except for a Moleskine notebook, a photo frame, and a small varnished wooden box with brass hinges and a brass handle on the lid. To the right of the desk was a table with a large-scale map of the lake spread out and pinned down at the corners with paperweights. On the other side of the room was a tall wooden cabinet, like a wardrobe, and some bookshelves. The wall opposite Tom, behind the desk, was taken up by a wall-to-ceiling window, which framed a view of Sour Hollow Crag, brooding over Hollowdale's grey and misty gullies, like a black-and-white photograph.

'Spectacular, isn't it?'

Tom swivelled around to see Rufus Clay standing by the door.

'I had to have the desk positioned with my back to the window, because I found such a beautiful view distracted me from my work.' He spoke in a calm, deliberate manner, like someone used to being listened to by intelligent people. 'Tom Hopkins, I believe?' He came towards Tom, and held out his hand. Tom instantly wished he had not shaken it, but it was too late. Rufus Clay walked round to the other side of the desk and sank into the swivel chair.

'Good to meet you, Tom. Very good to meet you.'

Close up, Rufus Clay looked as unlike a psychopath as it was possible to imagine and, not for the first time in recent days, Tom found himself questioning his own grasp of reality. He was tall, with a reddish, slightly puffy complexion, and a full head of white hair, neatly cut. Wearing a grey suit and a pale yellow shirt, without a tie, his hands clasped loosely together in front of him, an open, intelligent expression on his face, he could have been a head teacher having a chat with a struggling student, or a vicar about to offer advice to a parishioner. Tom found himself wondering what was in the photo frame on the desk. Would it be family, children, friends, a cat?

But then, as he opened the notebook and smoothed the page flat with the back of a hand, Tom caught a glimpse of a tattoo on the back of his wrist: the winged messenger! Tom remembered the photograph of the group of soldiers they had found on the internet. Experts in electronic warfare. No, it was real. Here was the mastermind behind it all.

'I want to apologize for this –' Rufus Clay looked at the ceiling, searching for the word – 'inconvenience.

Right at the beginning of your summer holidays too. But we can make this as painless as you like.'

'What do you want?' Tom's throat was dry and his voice sounded reedy. He grabbed hold of the arms of his chair with both hands and tried to breathe steadily. Somehow he had to gather his wits.

'You rumbled us, Tom. And that is very impressive. Because no one else did. And I mean *no one*.' He pulled a pen from his jacket pocket and held it poised over the notebook, like a waiter ready to take an order. 'So I need to know how you knew about us, and to whom you have spoken about us, that's all. Once you have explained that to my satisfaction, this process can come to an end.'

Tom shrugged and tried to look confused. 'Knew about you? How do you mean?'

Rufus Clay smiled and wagged a finger at him. 'OK. Let's make this simple. Why don't we go for yes-and-no-type questions? So. Did you or did you not *heroically* save the Queen's life on Wednesday by ensuring that the vessel she was aboard, in avoiding a collision with yours, unwittingly took evasive action from an aerial attack by Unmanned Aerial Vehicles camouflaged as birds? Yes or no?' He raised his eyebrows, waiting for an answer.

Tom felt like a criminal in the dock being interrogated by a brilliant barrister. He looked at the table and imagined, as he had done many times before, his father being questioned somewhere in a windowless room: the bare bulb swinging above a table, the slam of metal doors. How would he have handled it? Would he have given in or held out, no matter what they did to him? Tom felt sure he knew the answer.

He looked Rufus Clay in the eye. 'I don't know what you're talking about.'

'That's the spirit! I like someone with a bit of bottle. So few young people these days seem to have any resilience. Good for you, young man. Good for you.' He paused and flicked through the notebook. 'But please do not lie to me, Tom.'

The very quiet way he said this made Tom start. Rufus Clay noticed, and raised his palms disarmingly. 'Look, Tom,' he continued, 'I have absolutely no gripe against Her Majesty. Or the Duke of Lancaster, as we like to call her affectionately around here. And thanks to you, she lives. But what I need you to tell me is how you worked it out. The Queen is one of the most protected individuals on the planet. And the best intelligence agencies in the world – I ought to know, as I was one of them once – knew nothing at all. But a thirteen-year-old boy with a limp and a boat called *Maggot* knew all about it? Now, either I made a schoolboy error in my planning, or –' he folded his hands in his lap and smiled – 'or you are quite a remarkable schoolboy!'

Tom's mind was in turmoil. Even if he told the truth, would they let him go, now he had seen what he had seen? The only thing he could do was buy himself some time. The longer he kept them guessing the better.

Rufus Clay looked at his watch. 'No rush, Tom. I do have an important meeting at eight o'clock, but until then I'm at your disposal.'

'I worked it out,' Tom said, shrugging again. 'Guess-work, really. I'm into birds, you see. I happened to be on the lake to see the Queen, like everyone else. I saw the seagulls circling down and thought they were behaving strangely. You know, unnaturally. And I . . . I just put two and two together. It was a spur of the moment thing.'

Tom let out a silent breath, relieved he'd found his voice. He thought he'd sounded convincing.

'I see.' Rufus Clay made a steeple with the tips of his fingers and looked at Tom over the rims of his glasses. 'The problem, my dear boy, is that the version of events you have given me does not fit with events as I saw them unfold. On the contrary, I saw you emerge rapidly from the river mouth and speed across the lake, looking for a way through the security cordon. That didn't look like a spur of the moment decision to me. It looked like some-one acting with great purpose on the basis of some accurate information. And I must know, Tom, where that information came from.'

Tom opened his mouth to speak, but Rufus Clay held a palm up to silence him. His face was set like rock, though Tom thought he saw the faintest quiver on his top lip, as if there was some pool of rage under the surface trying to escape. Tom knew that he had to escape before it had a chance.

CHAPTER 29

Maggie got to work pitching the tent, while Joel disappeared into the trees to gather firewood, Archie dashing ahead, nose pressed to the ground. The tarn was surrounded by boggy pools dotted with sedge and long grasses, and the only firm place to make a camp was on the embankment of a slow-flowing stream that emptied into the tarn alongside a narrow spit. Maggie found some large stones in the stream and arranged them in a circle for a fire. She felt a raindrop on her head and looked up to see a bank of heavy clouds barrelling in from the north.

'Look what Archie sniffed out,' called Joel, returning

breathlessly from the trees. He held something triumphantly in the air. In his hand was what appeared to be the remains of a bird that had been torn apart by a fox. On closer inspection, what looked like a wing was a piece of plastic, edged with grey feathers, and where there should have been a mess of veins and bone and cartilage was a tangle of coloured wires and twisted aluminium.

'A piece of bird drone!' said Maggie.

'A piece of a rudder disguised as a tail, to be precise. This proves we're on the right track. They must have been flight-testing them and one crashed into the trees and broke up. Someone obviously came to retrieve it but didn't get every bit. I followed the tracks for a little way and there's no doubt that they came from over the ridge.'

Maggie grabbed his arm. 'What if they see us here?'

'It doesn't matter if they do. We just look like some campers, don't we?'

Maggie looked at the little tent with its neat fire by the stream. 'I suppose so.'

'Let's get up to the ridge and have a look at the place,' said Joel.

They closed up the tent and plunged into the thickly planted conifers, stooping under low branches and scratching their heads on twigs. At times they were almost crawling over the carpet of needles. They came out into the open again so suddenly it was as if the wood had spat them out, and then the ridge was right in front of them. This was steeper than it had looked from below, and they fell silent as they searched for hand-and-foot holds in the near-vertical rock, hoisting themselves over boulders and through crevices until they emerged, panting, on to the crest of a limestone escarpment.

Maggie felt a rush of wind in her hair as she looked out over a deep, empty gorge. Directly below them, the escarpment gave way to loose scree, which bottomed out in a gentle curve, studded with sheep half-lost in bracken. An insignificant beck wound its way along the valley floor and on the other side of this a rutted track clung to the fellside for a while before plunging out of sight towards the main road. Across the valley was a rambling cluster of buildings, squat and grey.

'It just looks like an ordinary farm,' said Maggie.

'From a distance,' said Joel. He had taken out his binoculars and was scanning the farm slowly. 'Let's see: some four-wheel drives, a quad bike, one of those yellow dump truck things, the sort you see in building sites. And there's the ice cream van. Nothing unusual in that. But how many farms do you know that are surrounded by razor wire fences? And have men with guns standing guard? And . . .'

His head moved in a circle as he followed something around the edge of the farm.

'. . . spy drones guarding their perimeters?'

Maggie took the binoculars and when she had focused the lenses she could see a raven-sized multirotor flying in a rectangular circuit around the edge of the farm. 'It looks more like a prison camp than a farm.'

'Or a terrorist HQ,' said Joel.

They lay on the sloping ground, leaning on their elbows, with their heads above the ridge and watched the place without speaking. A buzzard mewed somewhere in the air above them. Joel pulled a tuft of grass up and threw it over the ridge and the wind blew it straight back over his shoulder.

The light was fading fast and a fine drizzle was beginning to fall. 'I think we should get back to the tent before we get soaked. Let's get that campfire lit. We may as well keep warm while we think of a plan.'

By the time they had a fire going, wisps of cloud were rolling over the ridge, licking the edge of the forest. They huddled close to the fire and ate chicken curry out of tins heated over the flames. The sound of a distant chainsaw was coming from the woods below.

'So,' said Joel. He didn't need to elaborate.

'I guess we could just walk up to the gates and ask to buy some ice cream and see what happens?' said Maggie doubtfully.

'Or,' said Joel, 'we could scale the fence and break in, find Tom, get us all past the guards and get him out?'

'Off you go, then, Johnny English!' said Maggie, laughing. 'I'll stay here and watch.'

The sound of the chainsaw was closer. She poked the fire with a stick, sending a column of sparks into the black above. 'Strange time to be chopping down trees.'

Joel suddenly looked panic-stricken. 'Those aren't chainsaws! They're motorbikes. And they're getting closer.'

They listened to the hoarse engines echoing through the trees. The drizzle had turned to a steady rain. The engines were roaring now somewhere close, bursts of sound on the fringes of the forest.

'Shall we make a run for it?' Maggie yelled.

It was too late. Three headlights were beaming into the rain from the edge of the wood. Maggie held an arm in front of her face to stop herself being dazzled as three dirt bikes slewed along the embankment towards them. The bikes skidded to a stop in a semicircle around them, hemming Maggie and Joel in, their backs to the tarn, so close the exhaust fumes burnt their throats.

CHAPTER 30

Rufus Clay pushed his glasses firmly on to his face and waited for Tom to speak. He'd said he had a meeting to go to. Tom had to keep the conversation going till he left.

'Why do you want to kill the Queen anyway?'

'Ah, motives!' He smiled. 'People go on about motives, as if that explains everything.' Rufus Clay leant back in his chair with his hands behind his head, looking at the ceiling. He sucked his teeth for a moment, as if trying to decide something. 'OK, why not? It can't do any harm, I suppose.'

Tom said nothing, but he was relieved at the change

of tack and found himself wanting to know.

'You will no doubt have assumed that we are your typical common or garden terrorists, with some kind of *cause*. An axe to grind against the British government, or the entire western world, or some wretched "ideology" they insist everyone should follow. Yes?'

Tom nodded.

'Boring!' said Rufus Clay, shaking his head. 'Boring, tedious and dull. And stupid too, if you think about it. How can you win people round to your cause by terrorizing them? No, no. Some might call me a mercenary, but that's a little pejorative. Really, Tom, I'm just a humble salesman. After leaving the army, I worked for a telecoms company for a while. But it was, quite frankly, *unfulfilling*. So I began to dabble in a bit of trading.' He stared at Tom over his glasses, as if checking he was taking it all in.

'Trading?' said Tom.

'Oh, don't get the wrong idea – I wasn't selling crates of AK-47s to Somali pirates, or anything so sordid. It was top-end hardware that western governments did not want to see in the hands of certain undesirables. Submarine detectors, minesweepers, stealth systems, graphite bombs, sonic weapons. Anything that promised to give people that little edge over their adversaries. But more recently, UAVs.'

He looked over the rim of his glasses again.

'Drones, Tom. Drones. Oh, they are going to be big, you have no idea. And now we are developing tiny micro-drones that can be minutely targeted and are virtually untraceable.'

Tom glanced at his stick, which was leaning on the desk. He knew all about micro-drones, but he tried to look blank.

'It's a revolutionary technology that enables the kind of surgical precision we could only have dreamt of a few years ago.'

Rufus Clay was getting into his stride, like someone making a sales pitch.

'We do a range of antipersonnel devices that can target an individual with minimal collateral damage, as well as more powerful ones that can destroy buildings and ships by actually getting inside them undetected. All for a fraction of the price of smart bombs and guided missiles, of course.'

'And birds, because they are undetectable to radar?' said Tom.

Rufus Clay puckered his lips with a self-satisfied look. 'Exactly. No one sees them coming. Conventional radar, which looks for shifts of position, is not good at spotting slow-moving and low-flying objects. Birds give a further visual advantage in case they are seen. This is the future, Tom. One day, instead of cruise missiles blasting from one place to another with all that nasty expense and mess, there will be swarms of little drones with miniature warheads – chemical, biological, nuclear, take your pick! They'll be as invisible to the enemy as a flock of sparrows. They will come out of nowhere and wreak devastation with pinpoint accuracy. Which means that the theatre of war can be almost infinitely extended – into the heart of a city, into a hospital, into a school, or even . . .' he said, peering over his glasses again, and forcing Tom to look away, 'on to a boat on an English lake!'

Tom looked at his hands, trying to think of how to keep the conversation going before the questions turned back on him.

'But why the Queen?' he said at last.

'As I said, Tom, I am a salesman. And to sell things you have to advertise them. But how do you do that in my business?' He broke off in a chuckle. 'You can't simply bung these things on eBay. But everyone needs a shop window somewhere.'

'So it was all a demonstration?' said Tom incredulously. He thought of the Bentley in the quarry, and what Maggie had overheard on Benson Isle. It seemed like a lifetime ago.

'Exactly. It was going to be the opening of our little trade show. The meeting later is with some potential buyers. Honestly, Tom,' he jabbed a finger at the door and continued in a conspiratorial whisper, 'there's never been such a ragtag collection of crackpots in one place. ISIS, North Korea, the Taliban, al-Qaeda, al-Shabaab, and half a dozen African republics. That's why I had to buy an island on the lake as well as this place. I use it as a second rendezvous and delivery location. I'm selling weapons to mutual adversaries, you see. Some of them would slit each other's throats without hesitation if they came face-to-face! It's a great business, Tom, a great business. And as long as human beings want to kill each other – which will be for as long as they roam this good earth – I will have my customers!'

Tom looked at the man across the desk from him, appalled. 'But why someone as famous as the Queen? Wouldn't you have been found out eventually?'

'That's the thing, dear boy. Because she is so high profile, they would have given it their best shot. But if we had been successful that would have been a huge coup in proving our product's USP globally. I would have had every demented dictator and wacky warlord from around the world queuing up to empty their Swiss bank accounts into mine! Which is why I am so upset that you –' he searched for a word, rolling his tongue around the insides of his cheeks, as if tasting something unpleasant – 'that you *spoilt* everything!'

He looked directly at Tom and despite the calmness of his tone, Tom saw that his eyes were reservoirs of fury. Tom flinched, and heard himself say, in a pathetic voice that came out as little more than a squeak: 'I told you. I didn't do anything. I saw some birds. That's all.'

This was followed by a lengthy pause in which Tom could hear Rufus Clay draw in a long breath from across the table. 'Right ho,' he said, standing up. He paced around and then came back to the desk and rocked on tiptoe with his hands behind his back.

'As you might have guessed, I already know a fair bit

about *you*.' He pressed the notebook open with three arched fingers. 'Your name is Thomas James Hopkins and you live at Cedar Holme, Watertop, with your great-aunt who is now your official guardian. Your father was Wing Commander Anthony James Hopkins who served in the RAF but is now listed as missing, presumed dead or captured by the Taliban.' He let out a low chuckle and looked Tom hard in the eye. 'Which, let's face it, amounts to the same thing.' Tom dug his fingernails into the leather arms of the chair. 'Your mother died when you were two. So far, so tragic.'

He sat down again, watching Tom, waiting for a response.

'So I think you might be interested in the second part of our trade show, which is to demonstrate a rather different animal. *Larus* – the seagull drone – is the ultimate stealth system. It glides without a motor, making it totally silent and virtually invisible to even the latest detection systems. But there is always a small margin of error with gliders. Hence the need for multiple launch sites. *Falcon 03*, however, is a self-propelled tactical system, designed specifically to intercept fast jets.'

He suddenly reached for the polished wooden box and lifted the lid. He peered inside, like someone selecting a chocolate, then reached in and brought out a perfect scale model of a Hawk aeroplane in Red Arrows livery. It wasn't like Tom's wonky Airfix kit model – it was a perfect replica of the real thing, complete with RAF markings and a little pilot in the cockpit.

'Yes, yes, I think you will be interested,' he said, standing up. 'Watch, Tom, watch.'

Tom watched as Rufus Clay lifted eight more model aeroplanes from the box and went over to the map of the lake on the table, and arranged them on the map in formation.

'I love the Red Arrows, don't you, Tom? The pride of the RAF. And rightly so. As you know, the Queen's visit marked the opening of the Lakes Summer Festival. And the end of the festival – on Sunday at two o'clock – will be marked with a display by the Red Arrows over the lake.' He moved some of the Hawks over the map to rearrange the formation. 'Except this time they will augment their famous display of flying skills with a brand new manoeuvre.' He picked up three of the aeroplanes in one hand and clenched his fist around them. 'Right at the end of the show, three of them will simultaneously explode and disappear into the lake.' As he said this he hurled the three model aeroplanes to the other side of the room, where they glanced off the wall and fell to the carpet with a dull thud. 'It's going to be a beautiful display of *symmetry*.'

Tom forced himself to meet his eyes. 'Why are you telling me all this?'

Rufus Clay looked at him, blinking.

'You're not going to let me go, are you?'

He made a sympathetic face, head tilted to one side. 'No.'

'So why should I tell you anything?'

There was a long silence. Rufus Clay looked at the ceiling and scratched his neck with a middle finger. 'Right ho,' he said again, more to himself this time. He must have seen some flicker of fear flash across Tom's face because he held up a palm and smiled. 'Don't worry. I'm not going to torture anyone or anything like that. I don't go in for all that nonsense – far too messy. But I do have drones primed and ready that will sweep gracefully down upon your home, and the nice little holiday house next door, and blow them both to oblivion.'

He took off his glasses, breathed on them and wiped them with a tissue.

'Do we understand each other, Mr Hopkins?'

Tom hesitated for a moment, then nodded.

Clay reached under the desk and pressed a button. 'Good. Mike will escort you back to your room. And if you are not prepared to speak by the time my meeting is finished . . .' He stood up and went over to the tall cabinet, opened the door and pulled out a tie. For some time the sound of the tie flapping around as he deftly tied it, using a mirror on the back of the cabinet door, filled the room. While the cabinet was open Tom caught sight of a black torpedo-shaped object at the bottom. It was the size of a large fire extinguisher, with handles on the side and an enclosed propeller at the back. It looked like some kind of miniature submarine. Rufus Clay tightened the knot of his tie, shut the cabinet and turned back to Tom. '. . . I will give you your own personal computer screen so that the last thing you will do on this earth is watch – in crystal clear HD video, of course – your dear Aunt Emily, and anyone who happens to be living within so much as a seagull's squawk of her home, meet sudden and terrifying deaths.'

CHAPTER 31

The three riders cut their engines and got down from their dirt bikes. The smallest of them pulled off his helmet and stepped towards them.

'Hello again,' said Snakey. 'You should have listened to me when I said we'd find you. Hop-Hop-Hop-Hopkins isn't the only one to mysteriously know stuff.'

The wind was stirring up sparks from the fire and sending swirls of smoke along the ground before dispersing it into the darkness. 'You! But how—'

'I'm sorry, Maggie,' Joel was saying to her, despair in his voice. 'I should have worked it out sooner!'

'What?'

'Snakey never took the memory card at all. It was Tom's phone he took – from his boat. And we sent him the grid references to this exact spot. That's why they've come to get us, just like Snakey said they would.'

'That's right,' sneered Snakey, waggling Tom's phone at them. 'Scared now, are we?'

Maggie stepped closer. She felt like an over-inflated balloon.

'It's you who's scared, you little loser!' The words burst out of her, spit flying into Snakey's face, making him wince. 'You're a bag full of fear. You're afraid of anyone who's different. You're afraid of anyone who might be a threat to your ego. You think you're someone because you have two parasites who live in your shadow. But it's you who's scared, Snakey. Scared of being exposed as the pathetic little nobody that you are.' She kept moving closer till her fringe almost touched his nose, but he stood his ground. She sensed Sam and Podge position themselves either side of herself and Joel.

'And you know what?' Her voice sounded hollow, blown away by the wind, and her knees were shaking. She could feel Archie pressing his body against her calves. 'We are not –' she poked Snakey in the chest with a finger – 'going anywhere!'

Maggie fixed her eyes on his, looking for any sign of retreat, but she could only see the angry flare of the fire reflected in them. She could feel, rather than hear, Archie's steady growl in her legs.

'Grab them!' Snakey said.

She saw Podge yank Joel's arms behind his back. Sam did the same to her, but there was something half-hearted about it. Snakey walked calmly to his bike, which was the one closest to Maggie, and came back with a hefty motorbike chain. He clicked the combination lock round with his thumb, like some cowboy flicking the barrel of a gun before a shoot-out. Maggie willed herself to see him for the scared little loser she had just called him. But, as she felt the darkness pressing in around them, she couldn't suppress the fear that was tightening her insides, and she realized they were trapped.

Snakey smiled dangerously. 'Podge, Noyley, hold them down and I'll tie them together with this.'

'Come on, Snakey,' said Sam. 'We've scared them, like you wanted. Let's go home now.'

Maggie saw Podge glance at Sam Noyland uncertainly. Neither boy moved.

'Come on, you wimps,' Snakey shouted. 'Hold them down!'

Podge made a move to push Joel on to the floor, but Sam Noyland hesitated. It was no more than a blink – but it was enough. Maggie wrenched herself free and looked at him.

'Why do you do what he tells you? Can't you see what total muppets that makes you?'

Snakey's face was clenched in anger. 'Hold them down or I'll—'

'Or what?' said Sam, swivelling on his feet to face him, the awe suddenly gone.

Just then Podge let go of Joel and moved to the edge of the circle of firelight, like someone getting ready to watch a boxing match. His face was crumpled with confusion.

'Yeah,' he said weakly. 'Or what?'

Snakey looked at them both with disgust and reached down to the fire to pick up a burning branch. He gritted his teeth in pain as he raised the flaming torch in the air, and turned to Podge.

'Or I'll burn your bike, that's what,' he said simply.

Maggie watched in horror as Snakey began to walk over to where Podge's dirt bike was propped up on its stand. She had to put a stop to this before he set the whole forest on fire and alerted the terrorists in their farm on the other side of the ridge, or before someone got killed.

While Snakey's back was turned she dashed to his bike and jumped on. She pushed a button on the handlebar and the engine fired up. Then, taking a guess at which pedal to press with her foot, she managed to kick it into gear. The machine jolted and lurched like a frightened horse.

'Get on, Joel!' Maggie shouted.

Joel grabbed Archie with one hand, Maggie's neck with the other, and swung on to the seat behind her. She desperately gunned the engine to bend around the fire, a stream of sparks trailing behind. Podge and Sam were just shadows on her left, lost in the smoke. She headed straight for Snakey, who was rooted to the spot, his face melting in dismay, and as she passed by, she let go of the handlebar with one hand and grabbed the burning stick from him. Somehow, wobbling and skidding, she kept her balance, straightened up, and raced away along the spit, the burning branch held in the air away from Joel and Archie. Moments before curving away from the tarn she tossed it into the water and headed for the trees, the dark belt of the wood looming towards them, just distinguishable below the rim of sky.

They crashed through the first line of trees. She felt branches tearing her scalp, then the wood seemed to tilt and lift, the engine screamed, and as she hit the ground, everything was dark.

CHAPTER 32

Tom's feet barely touched the floor as Mike half-dragged, half-carried him back to the cell. They came to the top of the steps. This was the moment, now, before he was slammed back into the cell. He lifted a leg high and strode out into nothingness. He felt his centre of gravity shift violently and allowed his body to slam on to the steps, pulling the other man down with him, the stick clattering after. They landed in a tangled heap at the bottom. Mike was stunned, kneeling, eyes closed. Tom didn't take his eyes off Mike's face as he put a hand in his pocket and gently placed *Gnat* on the floor next to the doorsill, then inched away from it so that his body would shield the drone from the rage when it came.

And then suddenly, with a canine shake of his head, Mike was on his feet, spitting curses and yanking Tom up by the hair.

'You stupid cripple,' he growled, and shoved him back into the cell.

'I'm sorry, I'm sorry. I missed a step.'

'Shut up, you moron.' He was rubbing his elbow. 'I'll break your other leg for you, if you do that again.'

When his footsteps had receded, Tom touched his forehead and there was blood on his fingers. He wiped them on his T-shirt and took a moment to steady his breathing. Then he pulled the top of the stick away and twisted the metal sheath to expose the control panel and screen of the miniature drone. He peered through the bars of the door, pressed the start button and heard the rotor blades stir to life. In the few seconds before Mike recovered from the fall, Tom had placed the machine with just enough clearance from the door, but if it swayed during take-off, the rotors would hit the step and the drone would fling itself over and that would be that.

Gingerly, he thumbed the lever, tilting the blades slightly away from the door, then up it went, until it was level with the bars and he could feel the breeze on his face.

The staircase was unlit and in shadow, so he was glad he had built a tiny LED searchlight into the base of the drone. He activated this with a switch and could now see the staircase, grey and pixelated, on the screen. As he piloted the drone steadily upwards, the waspish buzz echoed around the stairwell. It seemed deafeningly loud, as if it were the only sound in the whole world, screaming to be heard.

It reached the top, and the key came into view on the screen. The nail needed to be long enough to make it possible to grab the key without the rotor blades hitting the wall. He did a visual check through the grille and the distance looked OK. Tom knew he only had one chance. Very slowly he inched the machine towards the key until the magnetic hook at its base made contact. Then, thumbing the controls, he edged it away from the wall and the key slid off the nail. Judging by the drone's sudden dip, it must have been a heavy key, perhaps thirty grams, and he had to almost apply full power to compensate. He held his breath as he brought it back down the stairwell until it was hovering outside the bars of the door. Here was the next opportunity for disaster. With one hand on the controls he kept the drone hovering perfectly still, just close enough to the bars, but not so close it would strike them. With the other hand he reached two fingers through the bars, touched the key with a fingertip, but couldn't fully reach it.

He had to fly the drone closer, but there were only a matter of millimetres now between the blades and the door. He edged it closer, jammed his fingers through the bars, and took hold of the key as tenderly as life itself. It was when he had felt the cold metal in his hand and landed the drone on the floor on the other side of the door again that he realized he had been holding his breath. He thought he was going to vomit. His hands were shaking violently as he put the key in the lock.

The sound of the lock turning was like an explosion in the silence and he imagined it reverberating throughout the building, causing the people in Rufus Clay's meeting to exchange puzzled glances. He listened, half-expecting to hear heavy boots running down the corridor. But the only sound was of his own breathing.

Before leaving the room, he unscrewed the light bulb from the middle of the ceiling and smashed it on the floor. Then he locked the door of the cell behind him and put the key in his pocket. The delay might buy him a few precious seconds. Unless he was discovered first. He stowed *Gnat* back into his walking stick and heaved himself noiselessly up the steps.

Tom peered through the windows overlooking the yard, where floodlights illuminated the spiralling curl of the razor wire fence that surrounded the farm. Somewhere out there were wide open spaces, brown soil soaking up soft rain, swelling the river that ran past his home and his family and friends, Aunt Emily, Jim, Maggie and Joel. And somewhere in an airbase many miles away, pilots in red jumpsuits were preparing for their next display, poring over a chart in a route-planning meeting, real people with names and faces and friends and families. Somewhere out there was life. In here was only death.

The right-hand passage led to Rufus Clay's office, so he turned left through a set of double doors, which opened into a corridor that was so bright after his cell that he found himself cowering against the lights, like a woodlouse exposed under a stone, his heart thumping. At the end, where the corridor turned a corner, was an illuminated green arrow sign, presumably pointing to an exit of some kind. If he could get out of the building, he would have a chance. Perhaps he could hide somewhere until the gates opened, but – he reminded himself grimly – at the speed he walked, everyone in the building would have died of old age before he'd had a chance to escape. Or maybe he could hide in the back of one of the vehicles in the yard? But then he remembered that they belonged to some of the most dangerous people in the world, so that wasn't so appealing either.

Before the corner he would have to pass an open door. The light was on in the room. He stood still and listened. There was a whirring sound coming from somewhere. He peered into the room and saw that the room was a laboratory, full of humming machines and flickering screens. There were tubes and wires everywhere. A woman in a white coat was working on a machine with her back to him. A strand of her red hair was blown out behind her as she worked on the machine, and he knew it was Victoria Juniper. Tom could see it was a wind tunnel, and as she moved he caught a glimpse of a brown-feathered wing in a glass tube.

He crept past the open door and cautiously rounded

the corner. The green arrow seemed to be pointing further inside the building. There were several doors on the next corridor, two of them wide open, and another green arrow at the end.

Tom peered into the first room. It was a small, square, windowless room, and seemed to be empty apart from a rubber mat in the centre. He was about to leave when he noticed a faint patch of light in the middle of the mat. He went over to it and looked up. Above his head was a stainless-steel chute coming straight down from the ceiling, like a chimney without a fireplace, and at the top was a perfect square of sky. A launch chute for vertical take-off and landing UAVs! He stood under it, numbed by the sudden longing to lift off into that moist grey sky.

He checked the corridor was clear and continued to the next room. This one was dimly lit and deserted, and he pushed the door and crept in. It was full of bird drones in various states of assembly. Some were bare skeletons, their electronics exposed like the giblets of a Christmas turkey, others were feathered and beautiful. Some were perched on stands, wings outstretched like exhibits in a museum, others suspended by wires from the ceiling. A tawny owl was standing in a corner, surveying the room. Tom shivered. The room was silent and still, and the lifeless birds gave him a feeling of doom, as if some spark of life had been suddenly snuffed out halfway through an act of creation.

Stretched across a wall, cables leading off from the feathered belly, was the stately form of a peregrine falcon. Tom knew he should leave, but he found himself mesmerized by the perfection of the thing, its yellow eyes looking right at him. He reached out to touch the delicately flecked leg feathers.

Voices jolted him into action. They were in the corridor. He looked around for somewhere to hide, the panic rising inside.

He squeezed under a laboratory bench as the lights came on and some people stepped into the room. Rufus Clay was speaking.

'This is *Falcon 03*, our fastest self-propelled remote attack vehicle. As we speak, Dr Juniper is making some minor aerodynamic adjustments in the lab, in preparation for our demonstration on Sunday.' He paused for someone to translate it into a throaty language Tom didn't recognize.

A dozen legs encircled the bench and faced the peregrine falcon. Tom could not move a muscle. From under the bench he could see several pairs of shoes inches away from his face.

'As you will know, the peregrine falcon is the fastest bird in existence, so nature has already given us the design we needed. The difficulty is getting propulsion without spoiling the natural aerodynamics, which obviously propellers would do. This is why, ladies and gentlemen, you will see a small rocket engine behind each foot. Once deployed, the feet fold up into the natural flying position, pointing towards the back of the bird, and the rocket engines come into play for the remainder of the mission.'

Someone asked a question, but Tom did not catch the words.

'Of course,' Rufus Clay answered, 'it's a tactical weapon, not a long-range one. But it reaches maximum speed in less than three seconds. That's why we called it *Falcon 03*. It can maintain that speed for about ten miles, depending on prevailing conditions. But its accuracy is its primary asset – as you will see on Sunday afternoon!' This was followed by laughter. '*Falcon 03* will easily evade the latest military and civil drone detection systems, making it, effectively, an invisible air-to-air missile system. This, ladies and gentlemen, is a game changer.' The translator translated again to murmurs of approval, and the group moved back into the corridor.

Tom listened to the footsteps fade and crawled out from under the bench. He checked the way was clear, then crept silently along the passage towards the green arrow. But now there were more footsteps coming from the corner behind him, regular and crisp, and getting closer. He tried another door but it was locked. He tried the next one, twisting the handle hard and leaning into it with his shoulder, but that was locked too. The footsteps were closer still, the steady clicking of heels, about to round the corner. His heart was banging in his chest as he scrambled to the next door. He fumbled at the handle, pushed and found himself falling into a small, windowless room illuminated by a dim emergency light burning above the door.

He closed the door and looked around. In the middle

of the room a machine the size of a small car was humming and vibrating. The door he had come through opened and a figure loomed in the entrance. He slunk behind the machine, crouching low, his heart pounding. He heard the door close and a light was switched on. Through the tangle of quivering ducts and pipes that led from the machine, Tom could see Victoria Juniper in front of a metal locker, putting on a quilted blue suit with a fur-lined hood and some thick gloves. She then went over to the far side of the room where there was a raised metal door set into the wall, with a turn-wheel, like the kind found on a bank vault. Tom guessed it was a walk-in freezer. She spun the wheel to open the door, and stepped inside.

He was about to make a dash for it while she was in there, when an idea struck him. It was a huge risk, but better than the alternative. He crouched low again and waited. Tom could feel his legs going numb. When the woman came out of the freezer several minutes later she was carrying an ice cream tub in her hands. To Tom's relief she took off her gloves and suit and placed them back in the locker. Then the light flicked off, and she was gone, taking the ice cream tub with her.

Tom decided to wait until the blood was flowing in his legs again before putting his idea into action, or he'd barely be able to walk. In the meantime he might as well find out what was in the freezer. He turned the wheel and dragged his deadened limbs over the sill. The freezing air burnt the inside of his lungs and made the skin on his face feel tight. The room was stacked full of ice cream tubs with that familiar colourful writing on the lid: *Luscious Lakeland – Real Ice Cream, Fresh from the Farm.*

He pulled a tub labelled *Damson* out and opened it. Inside was a pale white substance – nothing suggesting damsons. It didn't smell of much either and his finger met with a surprising resistance when he prodded it. He put the tub back and looked at the other flavours. Running from top to bottom there were *Apple Pie*, *Banoffee*, *Coconut*, *Damson* and *Eton Mess*. Tom stared at them. There was something too exotic about the selection of flavours. Why no vanilla, strawberry and raspberry ripple?

He was about to give up, when it hit him that the tubs were arranged in alphabetical order. Perhaps the flavours formed an alphabetical code, signalling the different forms of the stuff in the tubs, whatever it was. He began to back away with a sickening feeling. The warning signs on the back of the door confirmed it: *Extreme Danger: No Naked Flames*, and he realized he was standing in a room full of plastic explosives.

CHAPTER 33

Tom closed the freezer door, went to the locker and pulled the quilted suit on, threading his walking stick down inside one of the baggy legs, and making sure the fur-lined hood was tightly pulled around his face. It wouldn't make him invisible, and he would still have his limp, but it might buy him a few seconds if someone saw him.

Outside the room, all was quiet. He moved silently along the corridor and came to another door on the right. This was wide open, the room brightly lit, and he had to go past it in order to follow the green arrow. As he came near the opening, he could see a large man sitting

227

at a desk in front of a computer screen. The man glanced up, nodded, looked for a second as if he were going to carry on with his work, and then looked straight at Tom. He opened his mouth to speak. Tom stood still, knowing that if he walked his limp would give him away. 'Bit cold today, Victoria?' Tom nodded, the man carried on with his work, and Tom hurried on towards the metal door at the end of the corridor.

The door opened with a squeak on to a carpeted hallway with pot plants, and pictures on the walls. Another passage led off to the left and to the right a stairwell, faintly illuminated by a green arrow, descended into darkness.

From somewhere down the passage there was a tinkling of glasses. Rufus Clay was speaking. 'The basic system starts at three million dollars. Now compare that, ladies and gentlemen, for example, to a second-hand late 1990s Rapier, if you can get hold of one, and I'm sure you'll agree, it makes undeniable economic sense.'

Tom followed the steps down and came to a landing, and another green arrow pointing down a further flight of steps. A cold dread began to stir inside him as he realized that, far from leading to an exit, the arrows were taking him below ground. He guessed he would now be a full storey lower than the cell he was in before. At the bottom was a metal door with another green arrow.

When he pushed the door open, he was hit by a cold gust of air. He flicked on a light and almost crumpled in despair when he saw a tiny square chamber, doorless and windowless – a hopeless dead end. The room was empty apart from a metal chest about the size of a fridge, laid lengthways. He pulled his stick from the freezer suit, sat on the chest, and put his head in his hands.

He remained like this for a long time, overwhelmed with fatigue. There was nowhere else to go now. Once they found his empty cell the alarm would be raised, he would tell Rufus Clay everything, to try and save his friends, and swift retribution would follow.

He caught a whiff of that familiar scent again. Suddenly he was in the top room at River's Edge, Aunt Emily pottering about with a duster in her hand, arranging her Grasmere Gingerbread on the table, Saturday afternoon stretching ahead. That was the smell. The earthy, herby scent of lake water wafting up through the floorboards from the boathouse below. But how was it possible that he could smell it here in this underground room?

There were voices echoing in the stairwell. Two men.

Heavily, he hoisted himself up from the chest, flicked off the light and stood behind the door, but he knew it was hopeless. Boots on the hard steps were coming closer. He could see how everything was going to play out. He would probably be pronounced missing rather than dead. These people knew how to make someone disappear. He wished he could have said goodbye.

He was surprised to hear a scrap of cheerful conversation as the door opened.

'Too many pies, mate.' A southern accent.

'Shut it! It's a long way down here.' Panting.

'Well, when you've got your breath back, I'll talk you through the escape plan. It's pretty cool, even for Mr C.'

'Go on, soldier, I'm all ears.'

Laughter. Light on. Door pushed back into Tom's nose, back of his head squashed against the wall. A glimpse of a tattooed arm.

'The gear's all in the box. If the alarm sounds, we assemble down here. If everywhere is full of smoke, follow the green arrows, which will be flashing. We leave all the doors open behind us.'

'Why leave them open?'

'Spreads the fire quicker. Once the place is burning it's going to be like a fireball, all that Semtex. And we want nothing left by the time the pigs arrive. When they poke around, it will look like a factory fire caused by a build-up of gas from the ice cream plant. Which means, if you hang about upstairs you'll be toast.'

The other man exhaled and swore.

'Nah, don't worry. This is last-resort stuff, mate. It won't happen. There's no way Rufus is going to let this one go wrong. There must be twenty million hanging on it, looking at that lot of customers upstairs.'

Tom was aware of a bead of sweat forming on his forehead. Tortuously slowly it began to roll over his skin, down between his eyebrows until it was on the ridge of his nose.

'Then what?'

'We get the scuba gear out of the chest and put it on. We might not need it in the tunnel itself. The water level varies, see? Sometimes there's headroom, but sometimes the tunnel's full, so we'll be swimming underwater in pitch darkness. Not the easiest thing, if you're not used to it.'

Tom pressed himself against the wall. The bead of sweat was moving slowly down the ridge of his nose. He was desperate to wipe it away but he could not move a muscle. It slid further until it stopped, suspended on the tip of his nose, gravity willing it to loosen its grip. That dangling globule of sweat was all Tom could think about. In the irrational, paralysing fear of the moment, he imagined it falling off and hitting the floor at his feet like a drop of water on a hot griddle, steaming and hissing, giving his presence away.

But the man continued his noisy explanation.

'Under the box is the manhole cover with a ladder down to the aqueduct. The escape route is an overflow pipe that comes out through a culvert into the river. It's a drop to the right after half a mile. The outflow comes out into the river through a metal gate, which is completely submerged. That's why you have to mask up.'

'How do we get through the gate?'

'Whoever's first at the bottom of the culvert needs to unlatch it. We kayaked up the river last night – the one that drains into the north end of the lake – and I got it ready. Long time since I've used an underwater angle grinder. Anyway, then we scuba down to the river mouth, where the boat will be waiting for us. Full throttle over to the island to meet the helicopter, then it's *au revoir* England for a while!'

At last Tom understood why the *Invincible* needed so much power. He was beginning to piece things together and he could not help feel a sense of awe at the terrible genius of Rufus Clay. The location of the farm above the route of the Thirlmere Aqueduct gave the criminals their road to freedom if everything went wrong.

How clearly he remembered Mr Woodburn talking about 'the greatest engineering project of its time'. To his geography teacher it was another chance to waffle on about those ingenious Victorians, hewing rock with nothing but pickaxes, boring the longest man-made tunnel in the world right through the mountains, deep underground, at a perfect gradient so no pumping was needed. But to Tom, this artery of silent black water under his feet was the stuff of nightmares. And now he understood that, if he were ever to breathe the free air again, it was his only way out.

The men were leaving. 'Oh, and whatever you do, don't miss the overflow pipe. If you do you won't be able to swim back to it against the current – you'll be swimming the ninety miles to Manchester, mate. And you don't want to do that!'

'What, swim ninety miles, or go to Manchester?'

The door slammed and Tom heard their laughter recede up the stairs. He wiped the sweat from his face in the darkness. He was shaking so much he had to use one hand to steady the other as he reached to switch on the light.

CHAPTER 34

Maggie's heart was pounding against the carpet of needles. She sat up and blinked into the blackness, listening to the sound of her own breathing.

'Joel? Are you there?'

He answered with an owl call.

'I can't see a thing,' she called as loudly as she dared.

Suddenly Joel's face was illuminated like a ghost in the trees. 'Come this way,' he whispered. When she reached him, he flicked off the torch and the darkness seemed even more complete than before.

'Why didn't they follow?'

'Follow? Maggie, I doubt those three will ever dare to get anywhere near you after that! You were like a knight in armour, the way you were waving that branch around!'

'I don't suppose they'll be speaking to each other for a while either. Hear that?'

From the direction of the tarn they could hear shouting and swearing.

'Let's get out of here anyway,' Maggie said, getting up. 'Snakey will want his bike back.'

'Listen!' There was a snap of a twig nearby. They froze, grabbing each other in terror. Maggie held her breath. Then she felt a nudge on her leg as Archie snuffled around her feet. She picked him up and let him lick her face, relieved at the warmth of his body.

'Come on,' said Joel. Holding hands, they half-scrambled, half-crawled up the hillside towards the ridge. The ground became steeper and after a while they could make out the shapes of branches silhouetted against the night sky. Then they were out of the trees and a cool breeze brought them the vinegar scent of bracken from the other side of the ridge.

They were standing on the crest of the limestone escarpment, looking down, as they had done earlier that afternoon, on the valley below, which was now washed in soft-filtered moonlight. The tiny beck in the middle of the gorge was lost in moon shadow but they could hear it gurgling away in the darkness, carried to their ears by the gentle updraught.

'There are a lot of lights on at the farm,' said Maggie.

Joel raised a hand to silence her.

There were other voices cutting through the night. Men shouting, dogs barking, a clang of metal. An engine started and they could hear the spit and crackle of loose stones on tyres, as headlights swept out into the dark and disappeared down the track.

'What's going on?' Maggie whispered.

Hurried figures were moving around the floodlit yard, and torch beams were sweeping the ground around the farm.

'They're looking for something,' said Joel.

'Or someone,' Maggie replied.

From the centre of the farmyard four lights lifted off the ground and spread apart in different directions, like a firework in slow motion. One became brighter than the others, and Maggie realized the drone was coming towards them. She felt Joel's hand on her back.

'Get down!'

They rolled into some deep bracken and lay still.

'Keep your face to the ground,' commanded Joel, 'and don't move a muscle. I'll tell you what's going on. Tom must've escaped. And those guys are not happy.'

There was a shrill buzzing as the drone tracked up the side of the valley and drew level with them, a powerful searchlight fixed to its underbelly, hunting for movement. As it passed overhead Maggie could see every hair stand out on the stalks of bracken in front of her face. It didn't stop, but continued behind them, down towards the tarn.

'That would make sense,' said Maggie, thinking hard. 'I wonder . . .'

As they combed the valley, the drones were casting cone-shaped shafts of light through patches of mist. They moved methodically, exposing everything in their path: sheep standing mutely in the dark; stone walls; the grassy bumps of the limestone valley. Unless they could dodge the lights as they came, anyone out there would soon be spotted.

'Well, if Tom *has* escaped,' said Maggie, 'let's make sure we find him before they do. Come on!'

'Right,' said Joel. 'That means getting as close to the farm as possible. He can't have gone far.'

CHAPTER 35

The box was heavier than Tom had expected, and after shunting it to one side to reveal the manhole cover, he lifted the lid and saw the reason why. Inside was a pile of diving equipment: wetsuits, masks, fins, oxygen tanks, an assortment of tubes and dials, some rubber-coated head torches.

Tom stared into the box, trying to remember what caused the water level in the aqueduct to vary. Presumably rainfall was a factor. Or was it more about need? He wished the groggy feeling in his head would go so he could think clearly, but he knew that until he had the sky above and a lake breeze on his cheek, thinking would feel like swimming through porridge. For a moment he had a blank and couldn't even remember what time of year it was. It felt like he had been in this place for ever.

Tom forced himself to focus. It was August. It was the school holidays and that must mean less demand for water in Manchester.

Or would it mean more?

The fact was he had never been scuba diving and wouldn't know where to start. He picked up a head torch and pulled it firmly over his head.

The manhole cover was in a slight depression in the centre of the concrete floor, like a plughole at the bottom of a sink. For a moment he felt as if he were outside his own body, looking down, and he was a spider trapped in the sink, nowhere to go but down the plug to drown.

When he lifted the metal cover, the familiar smell of lake water hit him. He switched on the torch and the bright beam was swallowed up by a black hole that disappeared into nothingness. The light picked out a series of metal rungs that descended beyond counting and then faded into utter blackness. He rummaged in the box and found a spanner, which he tossed into the shaft. The torchlight picked out its spinning form for a few seconds, then it was gone, and sometime after that he heard the faint splash.

Tom felt something inside his belly twisting like cut glass. He knew he couldn't do it. When even an underground car park made him feel a silent scream rising in his chest, how could he climb down that ladder, into that great intestine that wound through the earth, billions of tonnes of rock and mountain weighing on his mind, and not crack under the strain?

That's what had happened that day in the summer term of his first year at the new school. They had been on the back row as usual: Snakey, Sam and Podge. As soon as he stepped on to the bus with its nauseating smell, Tom thought he would vomit, and had been given a seat at the front next to Manky McDonald, as usual, who chatted endlessly about Minecraft, as they growled their way up the hairpin bends towards the slate mines. But it was not travel sickness, or even Manky's smell, that was the problem.

In the car park everyone put their wellies on and Mr Woodburn handed out clipboards and worksheets and they set off up a winding gravel track between towering slag heaps of broken slate. At a narrow opening at the bottom of a wall of rock, they were met by some men dressed like miners, all hi-vis waterproofs and helmets and ropes. One of the men gave a safety talk and then handed out hard hats with miners' lights on the front.

After the muttering and faffing of getting everyone kitted out had died down, Mr Woodburn gave a little lecture about the importance of the slate mining industry, and everything he said made Tom's fear grow, like an animal eating him from inside. While Mr Woodburn praised the 'sheer grit' of the miners who had carved out these tunnels beneath 'millions and millions of tonnes of earth and rock with nothing but a few hand tools', Tom wished with every fibre of his being that the miners hadn't bothered, or that there would suddenly be a flood, so they couldn't get in, or that Mr Woodburn would have a seizure and need urgent medical attention, or that the bus driver – who had remained in the bus with a flask of coffee and a bag of doughnuts – would haul himself out of his seat and come waddling up the track with a message that the school was burning down and they all had to get home.

But none of those things happened, and they had all filed through the entrance, with one of the hi-vis men counting them in with a clicker, and Tom had found himself in the middle of a pack of shoving bodies, all *hoo-hoo*ing to hear the echoes, fifty feet underground, ankle-deep in water, stooping and stumbling through the clammy tunnel and all he could think about were the millions and millions of tonnes of rock and earth that those gritty miners had put between him and the beautiful sky.

He could hear Mr Woodburn up ahead calling cheerfully for them to keep up, but the pack was thinning out and he soon found himself some distance away from the person in front. He was aware of Snakey and his friends behind him by their constant prattle. He wished they were in front. He wanted as few people as possible between him and the entrance where, as he looked over his shoulder, a slit of daylight fell on the puddled water like a token of another world, and then disappeared as they rounded a bend.

Ahead the tunnel opened up into a cavern and the class had assembled into a hushed clump. Mr Woodburn made everyone switch off their lights in order to experience, he said, the sort of darkness they would rarely, if ever, have experienced before. Finally Mr Woodburn turned his light off.

'I've gone blind!' shouted some joker and laughter echoed around the cavern. But Tom pressed his hands on to his temples, begging himself to keep calm, telling himself it would soon be over and vowing to savour every breath once he was out.

The tunnel descended deeper. Further on there was another hold-up and this time everyone was gasping about a sheer drop, where the tunnel wall had fallen away into emptiness. Mr Woodburn was droning on about sedimentary rock . . . water . . . millions of years . . . and one of the hi-vis men was telling them to stand clear. Tom couldn't take in what was being said. He was looking ahead to where the tunnel narrowed to a hole no bigger than the entrance to a dog kennel. One by one, everyone was lining up to get on their hands and knees and squeeze, head first, through the tunnel. Someone was sniggering about Aiden Smith's belly getting stuck like a cork in a bottle, and suddenly Tom was aware that Snakey was right behind him.

'Enjoying yourself, Hopkins?'

Tom's stomach was clenched like a fist and his throat was too dry to make a sound.

'Not speaking? Just trying to be friendly, Hopkins!'

'Hey, Snakey.' It was Podge. 'I have a feeling Hopkins doesn't like it underground.'

'Scared of the dark?' said Sam Noyland, with a quiver in his own voice.

Then it was Tom's turn to go through the tunnel and Mr Woodburn was pushing his head down to get clear of the rock. He could see the feet of the person in front and nothing else. The passage was two feet high, floor to ceiling. He could not go on. He put his head on the floor and closed his eyes. He could hear Snakey behind him, but nothing went in. All he could think about was rock, rock, rock. Millions and millions of tonnes. Rock. Collapsing, falling, crushing. Trapped in darkness, no air.

Then he was screaming.

Many times later, Snakey would tell the world that he had been 'crying like a baby'.

His arms and legs were jammed. He wanted to stand but couldn't. He wanted to run but his legs were stuck fast. He had to get out. He wanted to strap himself to a stick of dynamite and blast through the mountain and out and up and away and above until the air grew thin and he overlooked the valleys and fells, and his lake with its islands and bays and wooded headlands, a dazzling silver ribbon, stretching into the sun.

He could hear Snakey hissing behind him with genuine exasperation. 'Move! You useless, snot-faced baby. You totally pathetic moron.'

Someone was holding his ankles, pulling him back. Then there was a light in his face, Mr Woodburn asking if he was OK, calming him down, telling him that he would wait with him in the gallery, take some breaths, then he would take Tom back outside.

But as he stood up his head torch had shone in Snakey's face and he'd caught a glint of triumph in his eye that he would never forget. He tried to push past him to get to where the tunnel widened, but Snakey was in the way, smirking. Suddenly the panic turned to wild anger, and Tom shoved the boy in the stomach with both hands. Snakey jolted backwards towards the wall, but Tom lost his balance, caught his foot on a rock, and plunged into the crevice.

He had come round in the air ambulance. His whole body was bound tight in a stretcher, his leg was in agony, both shame and anger fighting within. He opened his eyes to see a man with a red helmet bending over him, injecting his arm with a needle. Before he closed them again, he was able to move his head enough to get a glimpse through the window, and the sunlight filled his head like a drug and coursed through his blood and bones and the vibrations of the engine and the pulse of the rotor blades beat in rhythm with his heart and he remembered nothing more.

Now the memory of that day was like a living thing that mocked him from the shadows, awake or asleep, always ready to punish him with the fact of his own cowardice. And he knew it had finally won. Tom put the cover over the hole and sat on the box, waiting to be found, longing for it to be over.

CHAPTER 36

The breeze had blown the mist away and the pale glow from the half-moon gave enough light for Joel and Maggie to pick out their route. As they stumbled down the valley side they called Tom's name in the loudest whispers they dared.

'Let's hope those drones don't have night vision,' said Joel as they scrambled blindly down a gully, scraping their shins on bracken one minute, sinking their feet into waterlogged layers of moss the next. 'Or heat-seeking equipment,' he added grimly.

They were heading for a clump of larch trees that fringed the farm track. This was the only cover near the property and they figured that if they could get that far without being spotted, they would be able to take stock and have a closer look at what was going on. What had looked from the ridge like a gentle curve down to the stream, close up presented an agonizing series of obstacles. A drystone wall loomed out of the darkness and they had to hoist themselves over it with a clatter of stones. A shelf of limestone suddenly gave way to scree that twisted their ankles and made them stumble and shudder like drunks. A grouse blasted out of some bracken, making Maggie cry aloud with shock. The bird rattled off into the darkness and, in the hush it left behind, the buzz of drones seemed closer.

As the valley bottomed out Maggie squelched, knee-deep, into a bog. She pulled her foot out, almost leaving a shoe behind, lost her balance and landed with a splash in a mire of sodden mosses. She groped her way out, now soaked to the skin, and joined Joel and Archie, who had somehow bounded across on tufts of sedge, and were waiting for her on the bank of the stream.

Joel raised his voice over the sound of the rolling water. 'This is the most exposed part of the valley. If a drone heads this way, we need to play musical statues. Crouch down and pretend to be a rock. Let's hope they think Archie's a sheep!'

They began to tiptoe gingerly across wet boulders, ankle-deep in water that numbed their feet. Archie was already across, sniffing the ground on the other side, when the drone that had disappeared over their heads earlier now shot over the ridge behind them.

'Get down!' shouted Joel. 'Archie, stay!' Maggie had never heard such fierceness in her brother's voice. They crouched into balls, folded their arms over their heads, and waited. She held her breath. The scream of the drone cut through the patter of water on stone, piercing and urgent. It was hovering over them at fifty feet, like a hawk spying a vole by the roadside. As the beam of light began its pitiless journey across the stream, Maggie saw the black water at her feet illuminated green with weeds swaying in the current. And then she could have kissed the velvet darkness as the drone passed on at last.

Shaken, they splashed across the stream and regrouped on the bank, holding on to each other's shoulders in a scrum. Archie circled their feet.

'This isn't working,' Joel panted. 'We're never going to find him in this darkness. All we're going to do is get ourselves caught.'

Maggie looked at the ground for a moment, thinking. 'Well,' she said, kicking a rock with her foot, 'let's make sure we do!'

'What?' said Joel.

'Get caught. If we can somehow make them think one of us is Tom, we can divert them from hunting him and he might just get away.'

'Brilliant,' said Joel, nodding with mock seriousness. 'An absolutely sure way to get caught by murderous criminals ourselves!'

'I know, but what if . . . what if Tom never gets out of

there? We'll always live with the fact that we could have done more.'

Joel put his hands on his hips and let out a sigh. 'We'll need a plan if we do get caught.'

'Let's start speaking Chinese! They'll think we're tourists who have got lost. They'll soon lose interest. Come on!'

The ground on this side of the stream was dry and firm and they made quick progress over the sheep-cropped grass. Just before they reached the track there was a roar and they dived to the ground as a Land Rover raced away from the farm, its headlights dancing on the rutted road.

Two of the search drones were visible now: one to their left combing the dale head, and another hovering over the farm, where two men with machine guns were looking at a map in the headlights of another Land Rover. Away to the east a buttery light was seeping into the sky.

They began to walk towards the farm. The yellow dump truck that they had seen in the farmyard from across the valley was now parked at a slant on the edge of the track some way from the farm. When they came level with it, Maggie stopped dead.

'No way,' she said. She climbed up to the open cock-pit, and stepped back down smiling. 'It has the ignition key in it. This will beat running.'

'Maggie.' Joel held his palms out, anticipating the argument. 'It's crazy. We're going to get ourselves killed.'

'I can do it, Joel. It'll be like driving a car.'

'But you've never driven a car. The only thing you've driven is the dodgems at Blackpool Pleasure Beach.'

'And Snakey's dirt bike!'

'Look, they're all running back inside the building. He must still be inside somewhere.'

'Come on,' said Maggie, clambering up to the driver's seat. 'We haven't got a moment to lose. We need to draw them out again so Tom has a chance to escape.'

Shaking, Maggie adjusted the seat for her height, and quickly explained her idea. Joel lifted Archie into the huge tipping bucket where he stood on a layer of broken bricks, looking lost. Joel then headed off towards the farm weaving through the larches. Maggie turned the key and the engine growled awake.

A few moments later Joel reappeared on the track, holding a branch in one hand, which he began to use as a walking stick. His impersonation of Tom's lopsided gait – the drag of his leg, the severe dip of the shoulder as he placed his weight on the stick – was unmistakable. He went up to the gate where there was now only one man on guard, still standing by the ice cream van, but with his back to the gates. Then Joel turned round and began to walk back to the truck. Maggie watched him brazenly limp towards the truck as the first rays of sun broke across the fell tops behind him.

Then Maggie started shouting, 'Tom, Tom, there you are. Get in! Get in!' repeating his name again and again. She blasted the horn loud and long.

From the driver's seat the machine felt as high as a

house and the vast bucket hid the road from view. She pressed the pedal and could feel the power of it through the soles of her feet. Despite the lumbering weight of the thing, she was surprised how light the steering was and she edged out into the track, facing away from the farm and pushed the enormous brake pedal with all her weight.

Suddenly the farmyard came to life. People were spilling out of the building and jumping into vehicles, pointing and yelling at Joel. The gates opened as Joel pulled himself on to the running board.

'Fly, Maggie! Get your foot down. We won't be able to outrun them in this thing, but let's keep the chase going for as long as we can!'

Maggie pressed her foot hard on the accelerator and the beast jolted forward. It gathered speed and the engine began to whine.

'You need to change gear!' shouted Joel in her ear.

The clutch pedal was so stiff Maggie had to stand up to kick it down and the truck coasted for a few terrifying seconds while she wrenched the gear lever across. She lifted her foot from the pedal and the machine bolted away like a racehorse.

The track rose and fell as it followed the valley side. Maggie was rigid, clinging on to the wheel. She couldn't look behind. In front Archie rode the floor of the bucket like a surfer.

'There's a bend coming up,' said Joel.

She pressed the brake and changed gears again with a

crunch of metal. She leant into the curve, tyres scream-ing. As they came out of the bend, Maggie shot a glance over her shoulder to see one of the Land Rovers a couple of car-lengths away, black smoke blowing from the exhausts, and behind it the ice cream van. The passenger in the Land Rover had his head out of the window, looking through the sight of a rifle.

As they hit the crest of a hill, she heard a shot from behind. Maggie and Joel exchanged shocked glances. In the dip after the crest, there was another burst of fire and a whooshing sound overhead.

'What are we going to do?' screamed Maggie in Joel's ear. 'They're actually shooting at us!'

There was a clang as the bucket skimmed a stone wall, then they were into a grove of trees and, in the muffled darkness of the overhanging branches, more shots, and a deafening crack as the bullet hit some metal.

'Just drive, Maggie!'

Maggie looked over her shoulder again to see the Land Rover on their tail, the gun pointing at one of the wheels of the truck. Joel was leaning over the dashboard, reaching into the bucket, pulling out bricks. Then he stood up, idiotically exposed, his teeth clenched. He began to throw bricks into the road, aiming at the wheels of the Land Rover. Maggie changed gear and pressed the accelerator to the floor. Trees and stone walls flashed past.

Suddenly she saw relief crumple Joel's face and heard a screech of brakes and something popping behind. She looked round and the Land Rover was veering off the road, careening down a bank. The ice cream van was skidding behind it, its wheels locked.

'Come on, Maggie,' shouted Joel. 'You can do it.'

They came to a hill, steeper than the last, and Maggie could see the main road where the track joined it between drystone walls. A minibus flashed past, heading down the hill. If only she could make it to the road, she might be able to get some traffic between them and their pursuers.

She looked back again and now the ice cream van was right behind, swaying as it rode the lumps of the road. The passenger, Mike McCain, was leaning out of the window, a gun in his hand, firing at them furiously. A shot ricocheted off the steering column. Another hit a tyre, and she felt the machine lurch to one side.

Then Joel's hand was on the wheel, and he was screaming in her ear: 'Watch out! The wall, Maggie! Brake! Brake! Brake!'

CHAPTER 37

Tom had no idea how long he had been in the room, staring at the hole. Perhaps five minutes. Perhaps an hour. He was disgusted with his failure. He knew that if he stayed here the lives of other people would be lost. And beyond tomorrow, countless more, as Rufus Clay sold his special brand of terror across the world. He knew, deep down, that it would be better to chance himself to the cold horrors of rock and water than the cruelty of human beings. But this fear couldn't be argued away. There was nothing he could do to make himself enter that shaft.

Tom realized he was sweating and shuffled the freezer

suit off, throwing it angrily against the wall. As he did so, a button flew out of his shirt pocket, dropped to the floor, landing on its edge, and started to spin like a penny. He watched it spinning for what seemed like a lifetime, a tiny blur, spinning and spinning with an energy all of its own. Ever so gradually the button slowed, the axis of its turning becoming less upright, its colour separating from the pale fusion, as if it were asserting its right to existence in a fading world. At last, with a final elliptical sweep, it came to rest, and there it lay, a tiny pixel of colour in the grey room.

He crouched over the button without touching it, and he was overcome by the sight of it, and the flood of memories that it brought – this powder-blue speck on the concrete floor.

He remembered Maggie picking it up from the floor when he had just been knocked over by Archie. He remembered how she'd laughed, and held out the button in her hand. How she had offered to sew it back on. And how cold and proud he must have seemed in her eyes. He remembered how she had stood up to Snakey. How she'd got the anaesthetic. How she'd risked her life on Benson Isle. How both Maggie and Joel took him as he was. How they'd believed him. Then he remembered Aunt Emily and her endless patience. Jim and his kindness and his steadfast belief that Tom might just be right: that out there his father might still be alive.

He looked at Maggie's button now, and a light went on inside. *There is*, he found himself thinking as he put the button in his pocket, heaved the manhole cover open again, and began to lower himself into the shaft, *something even more powerful than fear*. He had friends. And he had hope.

But now there were voices outside the room, boots on the stairs, a radio crackle. They must have found his empty cell.

'Flamin' Houdini! How did he do it? That's the first thing I'm gonna get out of that runt when I catch him!' The unfit one from before. 'Mike swears he left the key at the top of the steps. And there's no way Mike would make a mistake like that.'

'Someone inside must have helped him.' It was the southern accent, the scuba diver. 'But who would be so soft in the head to do that?'

'Whoever it was, I wouldn't want to be in their shoes by the time Mike finishes with them.'

There was a voice on the radio asking for an update.

'We're in level two. Just checking out the escape chamber.'

The footsteps were coming down the final set of stairs. Tom began to pull the heavy metal cover towards him, but he realized he had left his walking stick on the floor. He had to climb half out of the shaft again, lean over and reach it. He pulled it into the shaft and let it drop into the nothingness below. It would be no use to him in the water, and if he ever got out of this place alive, he could make a dozen more micro-drones.

Now he was exposed, half in and half out of the hole.

He began to fumble manically with the lid, but it was too late. There was a hand on the door handle.

The voice on the radio suddenly came into the room as the door cracked open: 'All units: abort search. All units: abort search and convene by muster point. Fugitive has been identified escaping south from base.'

'Roger that,' was the last he heard from the men as their footsteps receded back up the stairs and he heard the door click shut behind them.

Tom exhaled and felt a shudder work its way through his spine while he processed what had happened. He could not imagine how they could have made a mistake like that, but it had saved him. Somehow, he'd been given another chance.

The rungs were cold to the touch. With one hand on the ladder, he reached up to pull the cover over the hole and, once again, he found himself swallowed in the horror of utter darkness. He could hear his own breathing, echoing, as if there were someone else beside him. But he had never felt so alone. He switched the head-torch on and began to move down the ladder. After what must have been fifty or sixty rungs, he stopped and shone the beam of light up towards the hole. At the sight of that cone of rock disappearing above his head he closed his eyes and clung on, the longing to be out growing like a bubble in his brain. He could hear the steady sigh of water beneath him. After another dozen or so more rungs his shoes filled with water, and his feet were being pulled away from the ladder by the current.

Bracing his body for the shock of cold, Tom lowered himself into the water. It was up to his waist and there were still more rungs to go. He felt the breath squeezed from his lungs as the water came over his chest. Only when the water was lapping his shoulders, little wavelets stroking the bottom of his chin, was he able to shine the light along the tunnel itself. There were eight or maybe ten inches of clearance between the water and the roof – just enough for his head if he kept his chin underwater and breathed through his nose.

He let go of the ladder and the current grabbed him and plunged him under. He came up again, spluttering, and the torchlight cast wild circles on the water that bounced on to the roof. He was disorientated for a moment, drifting backwards. He pushed off the wall with a foot and tried to steady himself with his arms, the earthy-tasting water stinging the back of his nose. Once facing the right way he let himself go, pulled along with the current, his legs tucked up under him.

What was it Jim had said? *Love is not a feeling, it's a decision.* He'd made his decision – to be swallowed by rock and water – and it felt like a slow death. As he drifted further into the deep earth he found himself fiercely longing to be sitting in the kitchen at Cedar Holme with Aunt Emily chatting away, pottering about, the washing machine swishing and whining in the background, the sound of the birds in the garden filtering in through the open door.

How many breaths had he taken in his life without a

moment of thankfulness? He wanted to sit on Jim's deck as a summer sun dropped behind the fells and talk about fishing. He wanted to take Maggie and Joel camping on Heron Holme, the little island at the quieter end of the lake that he had spitefully kept secret from them. He wanted to ask Maggie to sew that button back on.

Something was hanging from the ceiling up ahead. He shone the light in that direction, and felt the breath of wings on his scalp as a bat skimmed past. He was wondering where it could have come from when he saw the answer in the form of a pale patch of light rippling on the surface in front. As he approached, he noticed that the rough concrete lining of the tunnel there was covered in lichens and liverworts. He came level with the patch of light and looked up into a brick-lined opening twelve feet high. It must have been some kind of ventilation shaft but there was no ladder up. The metal grille at the top was framed by ferns and mosses and beyond it, the orange glow of dawn. It was like a summons from another world and he almost choked at the sight.

Tom tried to take deep breaths as he let himself drift off into darkness again. The tunnel was beginning to round a gradual bend to the right. When it straightened out, there was the sound of rushing water. It had to be the overflow pipe that ran down to the river that he had overheard the men talking about, a drop to the right after half a mile. The men in the escape room said it flowed into the river which drained into the north end of the lake. That was the Elleray. And Tom had a feeling he knew where it came out. If he was right, it was less than half a mile upstream from Cedar Holme!

If he missed it, it would be impossible to swim back against the current. He back-paddled with his hands against the flow to slow down. The sound of falling water was growing louder, a sheet of white noise.

Then he was level with the escape pipe. There was a metal sluice gate with a curtain of water rushing over. He grabbed hold of the gate and felt the force of the water pulling him away. He held on tight and shone the light over the gate. On the other side was a near-vertical fall. Without giving himself time to have second thoughts, he climbed over the gate and sat at the top of it, water rushing under and around him. The posture felt bizarrely familiar but it took him some time to think why. Then he remembered – he could have been at the top of a water chute on holiday years ago, screaming kids pushing and shoving behind him, butterflies in his stomach, then the bumps and bends and the triumphant splash, followed by the chlorine sting in his throat. But who knew what there would be at the end of this? All he knew was that there was nowhere else to go.

As soon as he let go of the gate the water enveloped him in its power. It slammed his head into the concrete lining of the pipe, then spun his body like a screw. The force and speed were impossible to comprehend. He was flotsam in a whirlpool. For a moment, as the pipe curved over like a death slide, he lost contact with the bottom, felt weightless for a split second, hit his head on the ceiling and then smashed back on the concrete bottom again, picking up even more speed, gasping for breath in the spray.

Then the gradient began to level off. Ahead there was a faint fluid light, but now the depth of the water was increasing in keeping with the angle of the pipe. This was it, the final triple horror: imprisoned, underground and now underwater.

Tom took a final gulp of air in the shrinking gap between the surface and the top of the pipe before he was completely submerged. The current pushed him on from behind, his head scraping the ceiling. When he opened his eyes underwater the green light was filtering into the tunnel from somewhere outside. He stretched out towards it, like a perch hungry for prey, and now he could make out the shimmering shape of an arch, the light coming through it forming a web on the walls as it shafted through a gate. The arch loomed into view, and then he was slamming up against the metal bars, grabbing them with both hands. With a sickening sense of panic, he felt their rigid strength barring the way out. He shook them, his sinuses stinging, pinpricks of light stabbing at the back of his eyes. He tried to stay calm but a terror was engulfing him. There had to be a way out. The men had said there would be a latch. He tore his hands free and moved them up and down the grille, searching the edges.

He could feel the burning in his chest, hear his heart thumping, see his desperate hands flailing in front of his face. Then he saw a metal catch holding the gate in place. He slipped his hands through the bars, twisted the catch firmly and the whole gate came free and fell away to the riverbed a few feet below.

Tom pushed out of the tube and up, rushing towards the light. He burst through the surface, grabbing greedy breaths into hot lungs. Oh, the kind, kind air, the rush of blood to the brain, light filling every pore. Like the first breath of a newborn baby, he coughed and spluttered and blessed the glorious sky.

CHAPTER 38

Tom lay on his back and let the soft current carry his body home. Water weeds caressed the back of his legs, and through the trees the morning sky seemed a brighter blue than he'd ever seen. After drifting round the final bend, he guided himself with a few hand strokes to the stone harbour at Cedar Holme.

He staggered up the steps and headed straight into his workshop. Everything was as he had left it, apart from a yellow Post-it note that had been stuck on the edge of a computer screen. On it was a message explaining that Maggie and Joel had gone to investigate the terrorists' HQ in Hollowdale, with a reference for where they were planning to camp. He slumped on to a chair like he'd been shot. He had to read the note again before it would sink in.

'Crazy!' he found himself almost shouting to the walls. Now he knew what – or rather who – was behind those razor wire fences, this was a disaster. Maggie and Joel were walking into a viper's nest. And after he'd just escaped from there!

He grabbed a pen, pulled a square of paper from a notepad, and forced himself to think. He scribbled a message on the paper, rolled it up tight, and slotted it into a small white canister. Then he picked up Uncle Ted's old landline that hung on the wall near the door, and dialled 999.

A few minutes later he was gunning *Skylark* furiously over Brockbarrow. He kept climbing until fells and valleys spread out like a relief map and the lakes were shining pools of light. At a thousand feet, he turned north-east and followed the bright strip of a beck for a few miles, then banked right and tracked across a wooded hillside, until he reached a small tarn enclosed with fir trees, a few wisps of mist rising from the water.

He spotted their camping place on a stretch of solid ground running alongside a stream. He lost height rapidly and hovered level with the treetops. Near the smoking remains of a fire, some vicious tyre marks told him all he needed to know. He desperately hoped he was not too late.

He throttled across the wood, past the tarn and over

the ridge, then plunged down the other side and began to cross the valley towards the squat grey set of buildings. He couldn't help breaking into a smile when he realized that evidence of his escape was everywhere. The gates were flung open, the buyers' cars had all left, a couple of men with dogs were descending towards the stream, flailing the waist-high bracken with sticks. There was no sign of Maggie and Joel. Whatever had happened at the campsite, he hoped they had not gone anywhere near the farm.

Then something in the sky above the gnarled top of Sour Hollow Crag caught a flash of sunlight. Another drone, a powerful-looking hexacopter with a bulky fuselage, was following the rim of the valley, searching the ground. He shuddered to think who might be at the controls somewhere in that building. He imagined Mike McCain smashing his fist on a table in frustration, and Rufus Clay, standing behind, calmly giving orders to find the fugitive at all costs.

He hovered, looking in all directions, certain other drones would have been deployed to search for the missing prisoner. But the sky was clear above the farm itself. It was now or never. He forced his shaking hands to relax on the controls, though his mind was in a frenzy. To reach Rufus Clay he knew he would need both speed and stealth – and a heap of luck as well. He cut the motors for noise, and angled into a steep, fast glide, looking for the launch hatch he had seen after he had escaped from his cell, like a buzzard hunting for prey. As *Skylark* circled down on to the farm, the shapeless grey rooftop began to separate into a jumble of gables and skylights, ducts and pipes. Finding that opening he'd spotted while he was inside Clay's lair was going to be impossible. He was at seventy feet, and the rooftop of the main building filled the screen with jagged angles and corners of slate and corrugated iron, but no way in. He would have to pull up, before it was too late.

Then he saw it. It was the slightest shift in the light hitting a flat piece of roof as he banked around, that gave it away. He turned, losing another thirty feet, keeping the piece of roof in his sight until he could make out a square of black. He pulled up, switched on the motors to stop, and dropped into the hole.

When he landed on the rubber mat in the launch room, he realized he'd been holding his breath. He filled his lungs with air, and headed through the open door. The corridor was clear. He ducked into the room full of bird drones. The peregrine falcon had been removed, but everything else was as he'd seen it the first time – the staring birds grimly tranquil on their perches and wires. He engaged the camera and took some photos. As they flashed up on the screen he thought they would stand a better chance of winning a wildlife photography competition than incriminating Rufus Clay as a terrorist mastermind.

He turned right and found his way to the top of the stairwell that led down to his cell. Suddenly he was back there, the green walls pressing him in, his pulse racing, and he had to take off his goggles for a moment, and gulp lungs full of air to reassure himself that he was several miles away in his workshop, and the police were on their way.

He put the goggles back on and continued from the stairwell along the dark passage with windows facing the yard and then retraced the route Mike McCain had taken him, until he was facing that single, unmarked door at the end of a long corridor. The door was shut, as it had been the first time. This was a dead end he had not thought through. To save batteries he rested the drone on the ground a few feet away from the door, and once again forced himself to think clearly. How could he get Rufus Clay – if he was in the room – to open the door? Then he saw the bare light bulbs. They were old-fashioned, glass types, hanging down from wires from the ceiling. He flew up to eye level with one of the bulbs, then edged *Skylark* forward so the front left prop hit the bulb. He saw the light go out, and, in his imagination, he could almost hear the glass pop and then shatter on the hard floor. He promised himself, when all this was over he'd build a microphone into *Skylark*'s nose cone.

The door swung open and Rufus Clay stood in the threshold, blinking. He looked up at *Skylark*'s buzz, and stepped out into the dim corridor, but as he did he stepped on the broken glass. While he looked at his feet Tom shot over his head, into the office, and landed on the big desk, facing the seat Tom had sat in.

Directly in front of him was the photograph in the

frame that he had noticed on the other side of the desk. It was a picture of a group of soldiers in brown desert uniform, fully armed, but standing in a relaxed circle. Tom recognized Rufus Clay immediately. A head taller than the others, a shock of fair hair under his helmet. Behind them was some kind of boxy concrete structure and a cluster of palm trees. They were gathered around a missile launcher the size of a pickup truck. Everyone was smiling at the camera.

Now, he looked beyond the desk, and there on a stand in the middle of the room was the peregrine falcon, stately and statuesque. It had a cavity open in its chest revealing entrails of bright components. The map of the lake was still spread out on the workbench, and the nine miniatures of the Red Arrows had been regrouped. *A beautiful display of symmetry*, Rufus Clay had called his plan to blow three of them out of the sky to sell his latest weapon.

Tom pressed a button on the control and took photos of everything he could – the map, the falcon, the picture on the desk. Evidence at last.

And now, for the second time in twenty-four hours, he faced the man himself. He looked as calm as before, but there was an uncertainty in his eyes. He stalked his way closer, wary but curious, step by step, to *Skylark*.

Tom flicked a switch to release the white canister. He saw it roll out across the desk and come to a stop. Rufus Clay reached out, hesitated for half a second, as one might before touching an electric fence, then picked it up, and pulled out the note. As he read it, Tom recited to himself the simple message he'd put on the note: *Smile for the camera. So far, so tragic. Tom Hopkins.*

Tom engaged the camera and fired.

To Tom's surprise, Rufus Clay simply nodded. The nod, Tom recalled later, was from the waist, not the neck, almost a bow, and the look on his face was a weird mixture of rage and something else. Acceptance? Admiration, even? And Tom was not sure if he had imagined it, but he thought he saw the corners of Rufus Clay's mouth twitch into the faintest smile. Then he walked to the cabinet, picked up the torpedo-shaped object, shot *Skylark* a final look, and was gone.

CHAPTER 39

By the time Tom made it back into the open, something was changing at the farm. The men with dogs were running back towards the fence. The drone that had been circling the valley suddenly dropped like a stone towards the farmyard. It crash-landed into one of the outbuildings and, instead of simply disintegrating, exploded on impact. Two more drones suddenly came into view from behind the dale head and they also fell on to the farm like bombs, each on a different building, each with a momentary blaze. The Toyota pickup that had brought Tom to the farm was slashing up the track, followed by two police Range

Rovers. The Toyota was a hundred yards ahead and made it into the yard as the gates were closing. The Range Rovers came to a stop in front of the gates in a plume of dust and armed police began pouring out and swarming around the fence, while heavy black smoke began to rise from the main building.

Tom began to move down the valley towards the lake, searching for any sign of the others. Emerging out of the sun haze above the horizon, a low-flying helicopter was making its way up the valley towards the farm. It was the Puma helicopter that had chased him from Brockbarrow and then jammed *Skylark*'s controls. As it passed to his left side he could see an open door and green-helmeted soldiers, guns bristling.

Tom knew they were too late and that the entire organization was being put into self-destruct mode. To the police watching, it would look like a suicide ending, but Tom knew this was how they escaped. He could picture them now making for the escape chamber, strapping on masks and tanks to make the long cold journey through the dark. The first down the culvert would be surprised to find the grille already removed.

It was then that he saw, where the farm track met the main road, that there had been an accident. Blue lights, fluorescent vehicle markings, traffic backed up on the pass. Nothing unusual on this steep route in the holiday season. It was the sculptured ice cream cone poking above a stone wall that made Tom take a closer look.

He pushed the control stick forward and accelerated.

Fields, walls, trees, rocks and sheep flickered in and out of view. In a boggy depression fifty yards from the road, a black Land Rover lay on its side, windows shattered. On the junction between the track and the road, the ice cream van had concertinaed itself into a drystone wall, and on the other side of the road a builders' dump truck was rammed up the side of a bank, its bucket hoisted vertically into the air like a sail.

When Tom recognized Archie, the jolt of fear felt like his insides had spun through a propeller. Was this how it was all going to end? With Maggie and Joel dead or seriously injured, and all because of him? The dog was being lifted down from the truck by a paramedic.

Then, when he saw Maggie being led from the truck, followed by Joel, the relief made him almost stall the drone.

But there was another figure he knew, crouching, alone behind the wall. He pushed the motors to full power but nothing Tom could do felt fast enough. The figure, bent double, moved along behind the wall to where Maggie was now being wrapped in a foil blanket by a paramedic. To get the right angle of approach Tom swooped past, indistinct faces turned towards him like Lego people, then rolled to the left, and backed around until he was behind the figure who now had his pistol raised over the wall, aimed at Maggie's head. He eased *Skylark*'s nose up to slow down, held position, lined the ponytail up in the cross hairs, fired a dart and saw Mike McCain's hand go up to his neck. He turned round, wide-eyed, to see *Skylark* right in front of him. Tom hesitated. If he pumped him too full the man might never wake up. But now Mike McCain was pointing the gun straight at *Skylark*. Tom looked into those remorseless eyes and fired another dart straight into his chest, and then another for good measure. He dropped the gun, and crumpled to the ground.

Tom pulled back a few feet, and saw Maggie's bloodstreaked face tilt up at the machine. She gave a wave in recognition.

The battery-indicator light was showing amber. As he climbed away from his friends, he found himself smiling, and then heard himself laugh out loud. He had forgotten how long it was since he had slept, he couldn't remember what day of the week it was, and a chill was seeping into his bones, but he had never felt so alive as now.

Just before the last rise before the lake, he spotted a boy trudging along the path, all alone. It was Snakey. Around the next bend were Podge and Sam Noyland, pushing their motorbikes. Tom found himself grinning at the thought that, by some twist of events he couldn't imagine, Snakey had lost his grip on his henchmen.

Suddenly Tom remembered that the drone was still loaded with one more dart. An intravenous syringe filled with anaesthetic, ready to sink into flesh at the press of a button. He dropped back down to the canopy, allowing the light south-westerly to take the sound of the motors away from the path. He inched forward until he had a clear view of that hot, red neck, and an intoxicating feeling of power swept over him like a wave and prickled his skin all over with goosebumps. This was the moment he had waited for.

He made some cross hairs appear on the screen and rested his finger on the trigger. He could see it playing out in his mind as he lined up Snakey's neck in the middle of the cross hairs. The dart would fly through the air, silent, accurate, its flight feathers in perfect balance. The piercing of the skin would feel little more than a wasp sting. A hand would swipe the back of the neck. Then, swearing with blurred speech, Snakey would slump to the ground. Beautiful.

Tom eased the drone closer, and as he did, he glanced to the south and picked out the shape of the long white steamer carving her way through the string of wooded islands. In the far distance the lake stretched towards rolling hills studded with whitewashed farmhouses, softened in the haze. The lens flared and fractured, and dazzling flakes of light like rough-cut crystals filled the screen. And, then, as suddenly as it had come, the feeling was gone. He heard himself exhale and lifted his finger from the trigger. A short while ago, he had been dead. In his own private tomb, with a few seconds before his oxygen-starved brain blacked out and his body was forgotten for ever in darkness, water and rock. But now his lungs were full of air, his eyes were full of light. He could feel the lonely years of rage melting away and he spun *Skylark* around and went in search of his friends.

CHAPTER 40

Tom would never forget the look on Aunt Emily's face when he walked into the kitchen, just after *Skylark* had landed. When she had finished hugging him, she stood back and looked at him, shaking her head in bemusement, and then they both burst out laughing at the amount of water that had transferred from Tom's clothes to her dress. Ten minutes later, Tom's clothes still dripping on to the kitchen floor, Jim arrived with PC Clark, who had shown him into the Toyota pickup truck at the police station. She listened with wide eyes and called some code words and a location into her radio. Aunt Emily insisted that Tom had a hot bath and a change of clothes. He didn't argue. But as he started to head upstairs, there was a roaring sound from the river. They all rushed out and sped over the lawn to reach the harbour in time to see an orange flash as the *Invincible* rocketed past, churning the whole river white. Moments later, there was a rumble overhead as the Puma helicopter appeared low over the cedars, and pursued the speedboat down the river. Tom, Jim and PC Clark got into *Maggot* and followed. They reached the river mouth in time to see the helicopter almost sitting on the lake, spray flying up like a tornado, heavily armed soldiers clambering down ladders on to the boat. Even at that distance there was no mistaking the lush red hair of Dr Victoria Juniper as she was hoisted at gunpoint, along with the others, into the bowels of the helicopter.

Tom had no idea how many hours later it was that he woke to hear Maggie's voice downstairs, as fresh and dauntless as ever. Aunt Emily had run a bath at last, and brought him a plate of brownies and a glass of milk 'to keep him going'. He slid into the water, felt the weightless warmth, and remembered nothing more.

Now, he woke with a start, the milk and brownies still on the side of the bath, and while he dressed he tuned into the conversation below.

'You should have seen him when he staggered into the kitchen,' Aunt Emily said. 'He looked like a drowned rat. All I wanted to do was get him into a hot bath. And it was all my fault!'

'How do you mean Emily?' said Maggie.

'I feel so stupid, letting Thomas get taken off like that by those thugs at the police station. I thought the police would have known if she wasn't a real social worker. Thomas was taken out to the car by the police lady, while I was filling in some forms. Then she came back in with this lady with red hair. She knew all about Thomas. Told me they'd take good care of him, and I believed her. She went off and I had to finish signing the forms. I came out to say goodbye, but he'd gone, and that was that.'

'Don't feel bad, Aunt Emily,' said Tom, as he entered the room. 'There was no way you could have known. And they were going to get me one way or another.'

They all looked up. Joel got up and high-fived him. Maggie gave him a hug. Tom looked at the ground, and found his throat was suddenly dry.

'You can say that again, Tom,' said Joel. 'When we were on the truck and Mike McCain was shooting at us from the ice cream van, he was only inches away from hitting us.'

'And only seconds away from shooting me after the crash,' added Maggie. 'But you should have seen him keel over when Tom shot him with those darts. Oh, and about those darts, Tom.'

Tom froze, remembering the anaesthetic he had persuaded Maggie to acquire from Mr Green.

Aunt Emily looked at the three of them over the rims of her glasses and made for the kitchen. 'I can see you three have a bit of catching up to do, so I'll leave you to it.'

'We've spoken to Dad about the propofol,' Maggie whispered, when she had gone.

'Yes?'

'We didn't have much choice, given that Mike McCain was found unconscious at the scene of the crash!'

'You gave him a triple dose, Tom, so he was like Sleeping Beauty apparently!' Joel added.

'And what did your dad say?'

She looked at Tom and grinned. 'He said, "If that's what it took to save my daughter's life, I won't be complaining".'

'But if it weren't for you two, I wouldn't be here now,' Tom replied. 'There was a moment when I was getting into the shaft to escape and they were about to find me. I thought it was the end. Then I heard a message on the radio that they had spotted me outside. I'm guessing that was you guys? That was my final chance to escape. And just in time!'

'What do you think happened to Rufus Clay?' said Maggie.

'The news report on the fire says that the owner perished with the farm,' said Joel.

'That's what he wanted people to think,' explained Tom. 'But the fire was not an accident – it was all planned as a way of destroying any evidence and allowing him to escape.'

'So you think he survived?'

'Definitely,' replied Tom. 'When I was in his room, right at the end of his interrogation, I saw that he had a tiny personal submarine. It looked like a small torpedo, with a propeller at the back. Designed to pull a single scuba diver along.'

'Cool,' said Joel.

'Then, when I went back with *Skylark*, I saw him take it out of the cupboard and do a runner. I'm pretty certain that while the others took their chances in the river he will have gone past the overflow and carried on in the aqueduct to come out somewhere else. Maybe he went against the current in the other direction. But he'll be miles away by now.'

The next day the interviews began. The first was with the local police, who were mainly interested in his kidnapping, how he had escaped, and how he thought the fire at the farm had started. They had also sent him away with a warning about breaking Civil Aviation Authority rules.

Then Tom, Maggie and Joel had spent the best part of an afternoon with a man and a woman from MI5, in which they had given detailed accounts of everything they knew and how they knew it. Yet, despite the mass of eyewitness details that they provided, none of it, they were told, would be enough to get the members of the gang who had been arrested actually convicted and locked up. The photos Tom had taken inside Clay's office were of interest but would only link Clay himself to any crimes, not the other members of the gang, and they were far from conclusive. Official records pointed to nothing more sinister than an ice cream factory, and every scrap of material evidence had been destroyed in the fire. Or was at the bottom of the lake, Tom had pointed out.

And this was the reason for the silence. It was an ongoing investigation, and they had been sworn to secrecy until further notice. The official story remained unchanged: a delinquent boy who tried to ram the Queen's boat, and the quick-thinking intervention of 'local youth Ryan Snaith'.

'Totally gutting,' Maggie said in exasperation, as they headed outside for some fresh air.

'Also totally understandable,' Joel replied.

But the last interview was different. Tom had been summoned back to the interview room alone, and he was told to wait to be discharged. He was expecting PC Clark to walk in clutching some forms. Instead a black man with aviator-style sunglasses, wearing a leather jacket over a polo shirt, came in.

'Hello again,' he said, as he sat down comfortably on the other side of the table.

Tom remembered the Puma pilot, who had chased and jammed *Skylark* on that Saturday morning. It seemed like a lifetime ago. He shook Tom's hand with a warm smile and introduced himself as Squadron Leader Richard Riley.

'Congratulations, Tom,' he said, 'and apologies.'

'I—'

'I'm not part of the investigation, you understand?

But I'd really like to know the whole story. If you don't mind.'

Tom hesitated, but then remembered the helicopter bringing the soldiers to the farm, and taking Victoria Juniper and the other terrorists away when they tried to escape on the *Invincible*. And so he told him everything. Squadron Leader Riley listened intently, eyes fixed on Tom, occasionally nodding or asking a question. He seemed particularly interested in *Skylark*'s role, and in the other drones Tom had made. When it came to explaining everything that had happened at the farm, including Tom's escape from his cell, using *Gnat*, discovering the plot to bring down the Red Arrows, and how Tom had escaped through the Thirlmere Aqueduct, he leant back in his seat and puffed out his cheeks in amazement.

'I wanted to apologize for not believing you when I jammed your drone.'

'It's OK,' said Tom. 'You were just doing your job.'

'But I wonder if the feeling was mutual?' He pulled back his sleeve to reveal the winged messenger tattoo on his wrist. 'You thought I was one of them, didn't you, which is why you didn't know if you could trust us? I was seconded to the Signals for a while, but I don't think my paths crossed with Rufus Clay.'

Tom reddened. 'I'm sorry too. Maybe if I had done, I would've saved a whole lot of trouble.'

'Maybe. Maybe not.' Suddenly Squadron Leader Riley leant forward. 'As I say, I didn't know Rufus Clay. But I

279

did know your father, Tom. Tony was my instructor. He taught me to fly fixed wings, before I transferred to rotary, and he went off to fly F3s in Iraq. He was a great man, your dad. He'd be very proud of you, Tom.'

CHAPTER 41

The following day, Tom heard footsteps on the gravel outside and Maggie burst through the door.

'Tom! Everybody's looking for you!'

'Just a sec.'

'What on earth are you doing now? Haven't you had enough of all that?'

Tom had his digital gaming goggles on and was making precise movements on the flying controls.

'Come on, we're going to be late.'

'I'm nearly there. Just one . . . more . . . inch . . .'

'We're all waiting for you at the harbour – Emily, Joel

and our mum and dad.' Maggie gestured needlessly towards the open door from where there was a sudden squawking from the magpies across the lawn.

'Ahhh! No!' Tom shook his head in frustration.

'Now you really do look like you're playing a computer game – and losing!'

'Gotcha!' he said at last, through clenched teeth. 'Tell them I'll be right there.'

Twenty minutes later they were all gathered on the aft deck of *Matilda*.

'Mmmm,' said Maggie, looking at Jim through a column of smoke. 'We could smell those burgers from miles away.'

Jim pointed with a pair of tongs to a basket on the roof of the cabin. 'Here, Maggie, if you bring me those rolls, you can help me put them in. Tom, how about you get everyone a drink? Nice bit of wood, by the way!'

Tom scrambled down to the galley to fetch some glasses. He'd cut a length of hazel from a tree at the edge of the garden to replace his stick which had been lost in the aqueduct. He hoped Jim was not going to make a fuss of him. So far he had been thankful that the return to normality had been exactly that. There had been no cluster of journalists waiting outside the house; no letter from the Queen to say thanks for saving her life; nothing public at all to restore his reputation.

When he came back on deck Jim looked at him and winked. 'He's done well, hasn't he, Emily?'

'All from the comfort of his workshop,' said Maggie, smiling at Tom.

Tom took a bite of his burger and felt himself reddening. Out on the lake the *Teal* was curving through a junior boat race, spinnakers ballooning as a dozen mirror dinghies rounded a buoy and started tacking down wind.

'You'll have to explain all that business, Thomas, dear,' said Aunt Emily. 'I knew you were an inventor, but I never would have guessed that you were flying little aeroplanes around the skies, spying on people and catching criminals.'

Tom found every face looking his way. They all knew by now about his traumatic escape through the tunnel of his own worst nightmares. He caught Maggie's laser eyes, which before had made him feel like a rabbit startled in headlights, but now he didn't look away. And with some surprise, he found himself smiling at the way things had worked out. Let the world think what it liked about him and Snakey. What did it matter? He had real friends. Snakey only ever had minions, and he'd lost those too now.

'We haven't caught them, though,' stated Joel. 'Not properly. It sounds like they'll get away with it after all!'

'How do you mean?' asked his mother.

'We lost the memory card. Which was my fault.'

'What memory card?' asked his father.

'Containing enough photographic evidence to bring the whole gang to justice,' Maggie explained. 'It got wet, and went missing while it was drying on the kitchen windowsill.'

'We assumed it was Snakey, Podge and Sam,' said Joel. 'But it turned out that what they took was Tom's phone. And that's how they knew where we were camping. We left Tom a message on his phone with the exact location. Another schoolboy error.'

'It wasn't, though, was it?' said Maggie. 'I mean, in the end?'

Her father looked at her. 'How do you mean, Maggie?'

'Well, if they hadn't tracked us down at the tarn, we would have slept peacefully through the night, and never have realized Tom had escaped at all. We would have woken up in the morning and we would have been too late to do anything.'

'That's right, Maggie,' said Jim. 'You were there with the distraction just in time. Even old Snakey had a purpose in the big scheme of things.'

'But,' said Joel, coming back, as ever, to facts, 'I'd give anything to know what happened to the memory card. If Snakey didn't take it, who did?'

Tom got to his feet now and coughed as if he were about to perform a magic trick. He pulled something out of his pocket and held it out.

'The magpies took it,' he said.

Every eye on the deck of *Matilda* now focused on the shiny square of metal resting in his palm.

'You get so used to them squawking in the cedars, you forget they are there at all. But this morning I was walking to the workshop and I saw one hopping across the lawn, and that gave me an idea. I made some simple robotic pincers and sent *Skylark* up.'

Aunt Emily picked up the little memory card between a thumb and finger and looked at it with wonder. 'So this little thing has all the information needed to put those people behind bars?'

'That's right, Aunt Emily. In fact, it has thousands of photos on it.'

'So that's what you were doing!' said Maggie. 'When I came into the workshop to tell you to hurry up. You were trying to grab this from the magpies' nest with good old *Spylark*.'

'Actually I had already got the chip by then. At that point I was trying to grab something else I'd seen in the nest.' Tom reached into his pocket again and held his hand out to Aunt Emily.

'Oh, Thomas! My engagement ring. Your little aeroplane got this down from the nest?!'

This was followed by laughter and applause, after which Jim served a second round of burgers and Tom topped up everyone's drinks. The conversation broke up and people chatted cheerfully, filling in the gaps about things they hadn't heard, elaborating on things that had already been said. Tom described Heron Holme to Maggie and Joel and promised that he would take them there and camp with them and they would make sure Snakey didn't come anywhere near.

After a few minutes, Maggie stood up. 'It's time.'

They put their plates and glasses on the cabin roof and looked out to where the sky met the serrated edges of the high fells.

There was a light southerly wind blowing, and the red ensign on the stern of *Matilda* snapped in the clean bright air. A pair of seagulls were wheeling over their heads, streaks of white against the blue summer sky.

Jim saw Tom glance at them. He caught his eye and nodded.

Then there was a burst of sound from the south. The momentary silence it left was like a vacuum, and then it came again, louder this time, as nine red Hawks screamed up the valley at full power, the surge of their engines ricocheting from the mountain walls and filling the air. Like a single machine with one mind, the planes tilted on to their sides and formed a perfect diamond, which tracked the length of the northern end of the lake, disappeared over the horseshoe of fells to the north for a moment, then returned and regrouped, roaring over their heads, corkscrewing south, red, white and blue smoke trails drifting over the water. No one was speaking on the deck of the boat, but all eyes followed the diminishing dots as they passed over the islands at Birthwaite Bay, banking and rolling, the sound now a distant rumble. Heads moved in unison with the jets as they formed a new shape and began to climb. Two single planes at the front, then two side by side, then another two spread further apart like a pair of wings, then three at the back like a tail.

'What are they doing?' asked Maggie.

'Blackbird loop,' said Tom. 'Watch, they're coming back.'

Faces were all turned upwards, as the group dropped into a near-vertical dive. They were right in front, over the lake, below the summit of Raven Howe, when they entered the curve and pulled up into a loop.

'Wow!' said Maggie, clapping.

'Carousel,' said Tom, as two planes passed each other at what looked like a few feet apart. 'It's the most dangerous-looking manoeuvre.'

'Champagne split,' he explained as the jets hammered up to vertical, then down and split in all directions.

'Ah, this is my favourite,' he said. 'The mirror roll. Two of them fly an inverted barrel roll with three others in formation. The minus G will be terrible in there.'

The houseboat was in prime position for the display. Out on the lake, yachts bobbed about, their sails flapping as every eye looked skyward. But on *Matilda* it felt as if the display was just for them.

'This is the end now,' Tom said. 'They're getting ready for the heart and spear. Two of them will do a half-loop with smoke to form a heart, then a third will come streaking across it with smoke to form a spear. Watch.'

The two red aeroplanes looked tiny as they prepared for their final manoeuvre. Then they were right in front of them again, red smoke forming a perfect heart as they each pulled into a half-loop. But there were four planes, not two, now heading towards the centre.

'Strange,' said Tom.

Three of the planes were diving vertically inside the heart, white smoke on and then off to create three vertical lines.

'They're writing something,' said Maggie.

Everyone on the deck of *Matilda* had their hands on their foreheads to shade their eyes from the sun. Eight of the Red Arrows had dispersed over the mountains and there was just one more remaining in sight now. It cut across into the heart. Smoke on, and off. On and off. Two horizontal strokes across the verticals.'

'They're saying thank you,' Maggie said.

'No, they're not, Maggie,' said Joel. 'Look, they've finished. It's a kind of thank you. But it just says, "*T. H.*" *Thank you, Tom Hopkins!*'

Everyone clapped and cheered. Tom, leaning on his stick, red-faced, made a bow, grinning broadly.

Over the fading sound of the engines, the cry of a gull could be heard as the valley and the lake with its sparkling bays and wooded islands and the gentle bracken-covered fellsides returned to their usual tranquillity.

'How brilliant,' said Maggie. 'The Red Arrows actually wrote your initials in the sky, Tom!'

Jim looked at Tom. 'Yes, it is brilliant, Maggie, my girl. But you know what's even better?'

'What?'

'He didn't need it.'

Tom caught Maggie's eye and they watched the sky

soak up the last wisps of smoke like a sponge. *How big and bright the sky is,* Tom thought. *How very bright and very big.* No, he thought to himself, he had everything he needed right here.

ACKNOWLEDGEMENTS

Getting *Spylark* airborne has been a thrilling adventure, the enjoyment of which has been deepened beyond words by the kindness and support of the amazing 'ground crew' who have made it possible.

I am very grateful to a number of friends who have read the manuscript, or provided encouragement, or just decent coffee, along the way. Thanks especially to Zachary Walkingshaw and Daniel Goody for being willing test pilots and enjoying the flight, the Heron family for sunset yacht trips in the name of primary research, and the Fortescue family for cheering from afar (I hope *Spylark* takes off down under!). I am also extremely grateful to Finn Sorsbie for visualizing Tom's world so helpfully with the map in the front of the book, and to Coralie Tomlinson for teaching me how to use commas!

I owe a debt of thanks to my parents for teaching me to love the lakes and mountains we were privileged to call our home, and to treat the written word with the respect it deserves. Thanks, too, to Rick for passing on the love of flying.

Although it is my name on the front of the book, writing a novel is not a solitary task, and no author could ask for more than the extraordinary privilege of being welcomed into the Chicken House team. I am very thankful indeed to my editor Claire McKenna for her hard work, attention to detail and kindness throughout.

It's also been a joy to work with Laura Myers, Lucy Horrocks, Elinor Bagenal, Kesia Lupo, Jazz Bartlett, Sarah Wilson, Rachel Leyshon and Rachel Hickman, all of whose expertise and wisdom I have hugely appreciated and learnt from. In particular, I want to thank Barry Cunningham for believing that the story could take flight in the first place. Having Barry's creative genius and enthusiasm on tap is a first-time author's dream.

Huge thanks are due to my family, for all the times I didn't make sandcastles, watch *Bake Off* or play Catan during the course of several years' worth of summer holidays and days off. As well as generously allowing me time to write they have enthusiastically shared in the journey from beginning to end. Thanks to Lachlan for unwavering interest and support, from that very first day, when – camping on the shores of lake Windermere – we gazed up at sunlit fell tops and a story was born, to the moment we rounded a bend in the river in our kayaks and knew at last where Tom Hopkins lived. Enormous thanks are due to Chloe, my first and most forthright editor, whose acute sense of story saved early drafts from a number of nosedives, and without whose wisdom the novel may never have found its wings. Lucy has been my most enthusiastic reader, and her beautiful, unfailing belief has been rocket fuel for late-night writing shifts. It has also been a joy to share the journey with Esme and Jack, who have patiently walked and talked their way around *Spylark's* 'three peaks' with me, revelling in the setting, as we discussed the latest plot point. Lastly, as with pretty much everything I attempt to do that is any good, most of the credit should really go to Emma, my wife, who keeps my feet on the ground, while also pointing my eyes upwards. With her, every day is an adventure, as we play our small part together in telling the greatest story of all.

Finally, a word about the setting. Just as most of the technology featured in the book already exists (or soon will), so the world captured by Tom's eye-in-the-sky is the real world of the beautiful English Lake District, including the three peaks, the aqueduct and all the bays and islands of the lake itself. To find out about these places, and more, see my website, www.dannyrurlander.com.

YOUR BLOOD WILL RUN COLD...

BELOW ZERO

DAN SMITH

BELOW ZERO by DAN SMITH

When Zak's plane crash-lands on Outpost Zero, a small Antarctic research base in one of the most isolated places on Earth, he discovers a cold, dark nightmare. The power's out and the people who live there have disappeared. Worse, as he searches for answers, bizarre visions suggest a link to something else – deep beneath the ice – which only he can understand . . .

Paperback, ISBN 978-1-910655-92-4, £6.99 • ebook, ISBN 978-1-911077-55-8, £6.99